MW01135643

ROUND THREE

BY

MÆRIS BLACK

KAGE UNMASKED

COPYRIGHT © 2015 MARIS BLACK
ALL RIGHTS RESERVED.

No part of this publication may be reproduced, distributed, or transmitted, in any form or by any means, without prior permission. For information regarding subsidiary rights, please contact the author:

Maris Black
Maris@marisblack.com

Edited by Jonathan Penn (Romantic Penn Publication Services)

Cover model: Mike Chabot

This book is a work of fiction. Names, characters, places, and incidents are the product of the author's imagination or are used fictitiously. Any resemblance to actual events, locales, or persons, living or dead, is coincidental.

This novel is dedicated
To all of the MMA fighters
Who risk their lives and health in the Octagon
& to all of the fans
Who love them.

1

(KAGE)

"KAGE, WAKE UP." Jamie's voice cut through my dream like a knife, sending the pieces scattering into the night. "What did you say you just did? What did you do to your brother?"

I shook my head and looked around. Strange window, bedside table, bed... I was on the floor. And there was Jamie, naked and looking at me with wide eyes full of fear.

"Jamie." I breathed. "Sorry, just having another bad dream. I didn't mean to wake you."

He opened his mouth, his lips forming words that were never spoken. In the gray glow of dawn, his brown eyes were warm and familiar. The only real comfort I could ever remember knowing.

I reached over and pulled him close, loving the way he folded against me. My sweaty skin slipped against the dry warmth of his, and I tried to focus on that instead of the horror I'd just woken from. It was enough that the dreams were coming more and more frequently, but now they were starting to take on the distinct feel of childhood memories. But they couldn't be memories, because that wasn't how things went down.

"You're almost as sweaty as when you had to cut weight in the sauna," he said. "But I don't mind."

He rested his head on my shoulder and dropped soft kisses there. I couldn't believe how tender he was, how his lips whispered over my skin, bringing me comfort when he could have just told me to shut up and go to sleep. For once, I was the child and Jamie was the mature one.

"I think I'm a terrible bedfellow," I admitted. "I've never really done too much sleeping with someone else. Not before you."

He left off with the kisses and leaned back to study me in the gloom. "Do you always have nightmares? Even when I'm not with you?"

I shrugged. "How the hell would I know? It's not like I can wake myself up."

"True. But have you ever woken up feeling like you just had a bad dream?"

"No. I don't know. Dammit, why the third degree? If my dreaming bothers you that much, I can go get a hotel."

Jamie launched himself at me, throwing his arms around my neck and peppering kisses down my cheek and along my jaw.

"What are you doing?" I growled, sounding more amused than the angry I was going for.

"Trying to keep you here," he said, earnest eyes locking on mine. "You can stay in my bedroom, and we'll just lock the door and have mad sex twenty-four-seven."

"Yeah, because I don't have a brand new UFC career to build or anything."

"I'll let you out for fights."

"We'd be at each other's throats within a week. I'm a moody bastard, you know, and I can get mean when I don't get my way." I was teasing, and he knew it. But both of us also knew there was some truth to my words.

"We've already been around each other twenty-four-seven at the Alcazar," he pointed out. "Do you remember me having any problems with it?"

"No," I admitted. "Neither one of us had a problem with it at the time. But it's different now, don't you think? Your job is over, and there's really no reason for us being around each other except for—"

"Except for I told you I love you. Do you think I would say that to someone I didn't want to be around all the time? I don't like not knowing when I'll see you again." The alarm in his voice tightened the knot in the pit of my stomach that had just barely begun to unwind from the nightmare.

"Has it been that bad since you came back to school?"

"Miserable." His mouth hinted at a sad smile as he tickled my arm with his finger, tracing the tattoo of his initials that I'd traced a thousand times myself. "Look, I don't care anymore about putting on a front or seeming cool or whatever. I've had enough time to think and mull shit over in my head, and the truth is, I just want to be with you. If you don't want me, then go ahead and tell me so I can start trying to get on with my life."

"You could do that, huh? Just get on with it?" I squeezed him to my chest.

"Sure, if I had to."

But I felt the truth in the way his heart pounded between us. He wouldn't be able to let go any easier than I would.

"What if I asked you to just lay everything down and come back to Vegas with me? Just quit school and move into the Alcazar with me, live on Enzo's cooking, lie around naked and look pretty… Would you do it?"

He contemplated for a moment, emotions at war on his face. At first he looked excited, his breathing speeding up and getting shallower at the same time. Then excitement gave way to disappointed resolve, and he shook his head.

"I've only got one year left, Kage. My parents have paid an awful lot of money, and I've invested a lot of time and effort just to give up now. I'm on the home stretch. When I'm done, I'll be able to get a really good job and support myself."

"Good answer." I rested my lips on the top of his head and smiled, breathing in his scent. "That's the responsible thing to do. We both know it, even if it's tempting to just say fuck everything and take what we want in the short term. You'd regret it for the rest of your life, though. The what-ifs would eat you alive."

"Gee, thanks for being my conscience. I *am* capable of making my own decisions."

"I'm not being your conscience, Jamie. I'm being the other half of a two-man team. Decisions affect the whole team, not just one member."

"A team? That's how you see us?"

"Yeah. Don't you?"

He scooted closer into my body. "I do want to go with you. I never told you this, but before I came back to school, I was almost ready to transfer to UNLV. I even looked into the transfer requirements and was in the process of doing research on it. But then Dr. Tanner told me not to."

"What?" I had gotten used to shielding Jamie from the harsh realities of my life, schooling my reactions, acting like everything was cool when it so very much wasn't. But I couldn't hide the shock when he let that bit of information fly. "When the hell did you talk to Dr. Tanner, and why would she tell you not to transfer schools? And for that matter, why didn't you talk to me about it?"

"I never got the chance to talk to you about the school thing because it was a last-minute development just before I left Vegas. You ditched me on that last day, remember? What was I supposed to do? From where I was standing, it didn't seem much like you wanted to hear anything I had to say."

That deflated me and checked my anger. "I couldn't do it, okay? Couldn't say goodbye to you. I was afraid I might cry or some shit. Fuck, why didn't I stay? If I'd stayed maybe we wouldn't have had to say goodbye at all."

Jamie nodded. "I was all ready to tell you, but you skipped out on me. Then Dr. Tanner showed up. She told me I needed to leave, that you were better off without me. She was afraid if I stayed, you would…"

"I would what?" I prodded.

"You would try to commit suicide again."

"What?" I repeated the word that seemed to have taken over my vocabulary. "Where the fuck did that come from? Commit suicide? *Again*? I've never in my life— Jamie, why didn't you tell me this?"

He pushed away, true anger taking hold of him. "Because you wouldn't answer my fucking phone calls, you fucking dick!"

"Don't call me that," I yelled right back at him, grabbing his shoulders and shaking him hard. "You don't understand, and I can't make you understand without dragging you into a lot of shit you don't need to be in. *Fuck*." I realized in that moment that Jamie was not going to let it go. I was going to have to tell him the truth about what was going on, whether I liked it or not. "Our phones are blocked, okay? And probably tapped. I'll prove it to you. Why don't you try to call me right now?"

He stared at me in disbelief.

"Do it!"

He cringed at the sharpness of my command, but he scrambled around for his pants and pulled his cell phone out of the pocket. I reached over and grabbed mine out of the inside pocket of my shorts. I held it up to him so that he could see the darkened screen that did not light up even as his end rang and rang. Then I returned the favor, calling his phone and getting no response.

"See? No calls, no texts. We've been cut off from each other."

"Cameron said you had blocked my number."

"I didn't block shit, Jamie. This is my uncle's game, not mine."

His eyes stretched wide. "What about the video of us... you know... fucking? Did you send that?"

Well, wasn't he just full of surprises.

"I don't know anything about a video, Jamie. Someone sent you a sex tape of us?"

He nodded slowly, then scrolled around on his phone. When he turned the screen around and showed me the detailed loop of us getting it on, my first response was nausea. Under different circumstances, it would have been hot as hell to see a porn video of us, but the fact that I didn't know who had taken it put a damper on any arousal I might have felt. It made me sick to realize that my apartment had been equipped with some obviously high-tech surveillance cameras. The picture was barely grainy, and the sound was clear as a bell. This wasn't some cheap nanny cam you could find at the security shop in the mall; this was some CIA-level shit. Even worse, the fact that it was a video of the night I took Jamie's ass for the first time indicated that we'd been watched for a long time.

Even as sure as I'd been that my uncle was meddling in the communication lines between Jamie and me, and that he was probably intercepting everything we said to each other even when Cameron had called my phone, I wasn't prepared for the mind-blowing effort that had obviously been put into the operation. Things were more serious than I'd imagined, and that scared the ever-loving shit out of me.

We lay there in silence for several long minutes, listening to the distant sounds of wee-hour traffic. Then Jamie asked the question I'd been dreading most.

"So what was your dream about?" His voice was wrapped in the most transparent attempt at nonchalance I'd ever heard, and the fact that he was concerned enough to try to act unconcerned put me on the defensive.

"Hell, I don't know. Don't remember. I can never seem to remember my dreams, can you?"

"Sometimes. Especially when it's a recurring dream like you seem to be having."

"Yeah? What kind of recurring dreams do you have?" The question was a way to get the focus off of me and onto him. Besides, knowing what kinds of things were created in Jamie Atwood's subconscious seemed like a new level of intimacy I wanted to reach.

"If I tell you, do you promise you won't laugh?"

"I don't know. I can't make that promise."

Chastising me with a lift of his brow, he began his story anyway. "The dream always starts on a cruise ship. You ever heard of that old show, *The Love Boat*?"

I laughed before I could stop myself.

"See? I knew you'd laugh." His bottom lip jutted out into one of his signature flirty pouts, and I resisted the temptation to sink my teeth into it.

"Just tell me the damn dream. I won't laugh."

"Anyway..." he huffed. "I'm on the deck of this enormous cruise ship, and all of these girls are hanging on me. There's no sound at all, as if the dream is on mute. Every detail of the ship is solid white, like a plastic model that hasn't been painted yet. Then as we're all just standing there on that too-white, too-silent ship, this barge comes floating by. There's a priest in a brown robe standing at the front of it. The only sound in the whole dream is the priest's voice as he reads from the Bible. I can't understand what he's saying, because it's in Latin or Aramaic or something, but whatever it is freaks me out so badly that I jump off the ship into the water."

"You jump?" I asked, more surprised than I should have been, considering it was just a dream he was talking about. "That was off the top deck, right? Do you drown?"

"No, that's the weird thing. I always expect to drown, but I don't. Instead I sink slowly down through the water, and I'm feeling fine, you know? I'm not breathing, but it's like I don't need to. After a while I see the ocean floor coming up to meet me, and I'm just sinking in slow motion. When my feet finally touch bottom, I get this tingly feeling that starts in the soles of my feet and spreads all the way up my body. As soon as it reaches the top of my head, I die. It's like I can feel death creeping over my body."

"That's disturbing. What do you think it means?"

"I think it means that I had a pointless dream once that was so strange it stuck in my mind, and now I think of it every now and then while I'm sleeping. That triggers it again. I figure every time you have a recurring dream, the possibility that you'll have it again increases exponentially. Sort of like how getting struck by lightning changes your electrical makeup, so that every time you're struck, you're just that much more likely to be struck again."

"That really happens to people?" I asked. "That sounds like one of those urban legends."

"No urban legend. It's science. I think some people eventually just become like human lightning rods, and it's only a matter of time before they receive the fatal strike. Look it up if you don't believe me."

"I'll take your word for it," I conceded, celebrating inwardly at how far we'd meandered from the original subject of my nightmare. Maybe if I tried hard enough, I could turn it into a political or religious debate. "Is that what you honestly think about your dream? You don't think it means anything, like you're looking for love in the wrong places, or you hate the church or something?"

He laughed. "No, Kage. I'm not that deep." He lifted up on his elbow and looked straight into my face, which was exactly where I didn't want him to look. "What are we even talking about? It's your turn. I want to hear about the recurring dream that makes my big, bad fighter cry. What's it about?"

Damn. So much for changing the subject.

"I don't know," I told him.

The pouty lip came out again, so hard to resist. "But I shared my dream with you."

"Mine is different."

"So you do remember it," Jamie accused. He sat up in the dark, haloed by the pale dawn coming in at the edges of his blinds, and stared at me like I was about to reveal the secret to everlasting life.

"No," I lied. "I don't remember it. And that's exactly why it's different."

"Come on, tell me. Don't shut me out. When a guy wakes me up in the middle of the night clinging to me like a little kid and squeezing the breath out of me, I think I deserve to have some idea of what he's dreaming, don't you?"

"Fuck off, Jamie. I mean it."

"But I want to know, Kage. Pleeease. I'm worried about you. It might help to talk to someone about it."

I rolled him roughly beneath my body and pinned his shoulders to the floor with my hands, putting my entire weight on him. "I can make you shut up, you know."

"I want to know," he grated, instinctively struggling against me. He couldn't do much, but somehow in his hampered flailing his hand scraped hard against my wounded side at the same time his knee accidentally found my groin. The searing pain in my side crippled me just enough while the nut strike was back-loading. Then the pain hit, followed by the sickness.

"Fuck." I rolled off of him, the combined pain of the two injuries causing me to writhe and blow out loud, shallow puffs of breath.

"Kage, I'm sorry," Jamie was saying. "Oh, God, I didn't mean to hurt you."

"I'm okay," I squeaked out. "Just give me some time. There's a reason they give you five minutes for a groin strike in MMA."

"Um, hello. I know what it feels like to get hit in the nuts. If you hadn't noticed, I have a couple of my own. Want me to kiss it?"

"I want you to stop talking." I clutched myself for a good minute and a half, breathing through it, counting the seconds.

"I thought you laughed at pain," Jamie teased.

"Not this kind." I tried to smile at him through the ache, which was now slowly starting to subside. "Besides, you don't want to hurt that piece of equipment. I do important things with it— things you might miss."

He ran a hand across my chest. "Speaking of things I might miss… do you think my friends suspected anything last night?"

I chuckled weakly. "I don't know. How drunk were they?"

"Pretty drunk, I think. That keg was dry by the time you got here, and I think they were smoking some, too."

"They were definitely smoking. I had to walk through a cloud to get to your front door."

"So maybe they didn't notice, right?" he asked hopefully. "It's not like we kissed or anything crazy like that. Or at least I don't think we did. Hell, I was so freaked out to see you, I didn't know what was going on half the time."

"Same here," I admitted. "But honestly, I don't think anyone caught on. And I was pretty subtle when I was threatening your *friend*."

"Really?" Jamie hacked out a laugh and stared at me. "You call that subtle? You picked him up by his collar, and then I jumped on your back. Subtle is not the first description that springs to mind."

"I meant the words, smart ass. I kept my voice down. I may have been mad enough to kill ten men, but I still kept it together enough to keep from screaming out our business." I bit my lip and hesitated before asking, "Does that make you happy?"

Jamie looked confused. "Happy?"

"Yeah, are you glad I didn't give us away?" God, I hated the way asking that question made me feel. Like I was a dog, ducking my head and waiting to be petted for not barking when someone came to the door.

"I'm glad you didn't give *yourself* away. That's what I care about. Remember when you told me you were the one with something to lose? You were right about that. You're getting famous now, and people are watching you and judging you. Nobody gives a shit who I'm sleeping with."

"You have plenty of people who care about you."

"Yeah, but it's a different way. A personal way. My love life is not going to make headlines on the sports blogs."

"Actually, it might." I pulled his face down to mine and kissed him on the lips. Those pillow-soft lips that I had missed so much.

"I'm sorry," he said, his eyes glistening with moisture. "For what happened at my parents' house. I'm so sorry. I wish I could go back and do it all over again. I swear to God, I would walk into that house holding your hand if that's what you wanted. I would kiss you on the lips in front of my parents, tell my sister to go fuck herself, and tell my dad you were sleeping in my bed. I'd do that for you if I could." He flopped over onto his back and sighed. "But it's not smart for anyone to know about us because of your career. *Only* because of your career."

"Are you sure that's the only reason? You're not ashamed of me anymore?"

"I was never ashamed of you. I may have been a little ashamed of myself for wanting you, but I was never ashamed of you. And I promise, if I wasn't so worried about your public image and your

UFC contract, I'd get on top of the Peachtree Plaza with a bullhorn and announce to the entire city of Atlanta that we're together. Better yet, I'd announce it on your website and social media accounts. You've got so many followers, that shit would be all over the internet within twenty-four hours."

"Hey, that's actually not a bad idea. Quick and painless, right?"

"Are you being serious right now?" Jamie scrambled up onto all fours and stared at me in disbelief.

I laughed. "Like a Band-Aid, you know? Just rip that sucker off, and it's done. Only stings for a bit."

"You can't be serious. I think maybe one of those times Diaz popped you last night, he knocked a screw loose."

I chopped his arm out from under him and toppled him over, climbing on top of him before he had a chance to react. I grabbed on to his wrists, one in each hand, and secured his arms above his head. "Are you challenging me, college boy? Because that's what it sounds like."

He squeaked out a sound that didn't suffice for an answer.

"You know what happens to bad little interns who get mouthy with the boss?"

He laughed and wiggled beneath me, wrapping his long legs around my waist and tightening them, pressing his hardening cock into my belly and positioning his ass right where I like it. "I think you'd better check the terms of my employment, Mr. Kage. As you pointed out earlier, my internship was officially over weeks ago. I'm a free agent now, which means I could sign with someone else if I wanted to."

"Is that right?" Jealousy surged through me at the thought of Jamie being with anyone else the way he was with me, and the now-too-familiar need to possess the man beneath me took over. "What about benefits? Do you think anyone else is offering such a substantial package?" I nudged the head of my dick against his hole, which he'd so strategically positioned, baring himself for the taking. I pushed hard, not trying to breach his rim, but definitely letting him know I was there. Wanting him to feel just what it was I was offering him.

His teasing expression melted into something much more primal, and he parted his lips on a breath. His eyes rolled back in his head before he closed them, his body going still and loose. The way he responded to me did more than any therapy could ever do. It was more than sexual.

"What are you thinking?" I asked, staring down into his serene face.

"Wondering where the lube is."

It took me all of four seconds to locate it where one of us had tossed it onto the floor near the bed, and to lean over and retrieve it. Then I was slicking my hand, my cock, Jamie's hole, and everything in between. I tossed the bottle, closer this time just in case, then I leaned back and looked down at Jamie all sinewy and stretched out. So trusting and willing.

"You'd let me do anything to you right now, wouldn't you?" I asked, my voice rough with desire.

Keeping his eyes closed, he wet his lips with the tip of his tongue and nodded slowly.

"You have no idea how much that turns me on— to know that you trust me. You know you shouldn't, right?"

"I don't care," he whispered.

I reached down and rubbed his taint, the spot I knew would get his attention. Sure enough, his eyes flew open and he started squirming, trying to get more stimulation. "There's that magic button," I said, rubbing it with my thumb. Then I slid my slick index finger up inside him, following the inner wall until I found his prostate.

"Jeez—" he choked out, every muscle in his body tensing simultaneously before falling nearly slack again. "Oh, God, that feels so good. Just keep doing exactly what you're doing." He reached down and grabbed onto his cock, stroking it like he was on the home stretch rather than just getting warmed up.

I leaned over him, and just as his hand hit the root of his dick on the downstroke, I wrapped my lips around him. His hand fell away, and he shuddered and groaned loudly as I sucked him off. I kept up the relentless massage with my thumb and forefinger, smiling to myself at the knowledge that he wouldn't last long with that kind of triple stimulation. I didn't want him to. Regardless of what my uncle had led me to believe, Jamie had been a good boy, and for that he deserved a treat.

When he came, he planted the soles of his feet on the floor and bridged up hard into my mouth, straining to give me everything and forcing me to take it. I just swallowed and swallowed, and stroked the taut globes of his ass as he shuddered through his finish. Then he lowered himself gently to the floor, turned over and curled into a fetal position. I wrapped myself around his body, determined to ignore my painful erection until later on. I'd show him exactly how much I'd missed him then, but right now I was content just to wrap him up and fall back into sleep.

No dreams, I told myself. *Not while I'm with Jamie.*

2

(JAMIE)

Emerging from my room the morning after the fight was quite an adventure. I had no idea what I expected to find on the other side of the door. Kage peeked out over my head, and after we'd both determined the coast was clear, Kage slipped into the bathroom with one of my towels. I proceeded on to the kitchen.

Fortunately, there were no party stragglers sacked out on the sofa or floor. The place was a wreck, but other than that, everything looked normal. I grabbed the coffee pot and filled it at the sink, but when I turned the water off, I heard Kage's loud curse from the bathroom. I'd forgotten that the shower water would scald your skin off if someone turned on the water in the kitchen.

"You just burned your boyfriend." Layla padded into the room, bleary-eyed from sleep.

"Oh, well. He could use some toughening up."

Layla pulled the orange juice out of the refrigerator, poured herself a glass, and leaned against the counter. Even first thing in the morning with disheveled hair, she was a sight to behold. A battered gray Mickey Mouse tee that was much too large for her slight frame fell seductively off of one shoulder. She smiled at me as she sipped her juice.

"So everything's good between you and the culero now?"

"If you don't stop calling him that, I'm going to tell everyone at school you have fake breasts."

"What? I do not have fake breasts!"

I shrugged. "I'm not above lying to get what I want. From now on, it's Kage or Michael to you. Got it?"

Layla's glass was in danger of breaking when she set it down on the counter a little too hard. "Fine. As long as you don't think it means I like him. I still can't forget how he treated you before, Jamie. I don't trust him."

There was that word again. Trust. Apparently it meant something very different to each of us.

Moving in close, I dropped my voice and spoke near her ear. "Just because you like things all nice and tame in the bedroom doesn't mean everyone does. Maybe you should try letting loose every now and then. Though now that you're dating Trey, that may not be an option. I'm not sure if he's got it in him to be forceful."

"Are you actually criticizing my boyfriend for being respectful of me?"

"Absolutely not. I'm just pointing out that different people like different things, that's all."

Trey appeared in the doorway. "Can't leave you two alone for a minute, huh?" He removed his round glasses and cleaned them with his shirttail the way he did when he was nervous.

Layla pulled quickly away from me and hurried over to throw her arms around Trey and plant a noisy kiss on his cheek. "Trust me. The only reason Jamie and I need a chaperone is to keep us from ripping each other's throats out."

"You got that right." I opened the refrigerator and gathered up a carton of eggs, a package of bacon, a jar of peach preserves, and the butter tray. Balancing the eggs on my forearm, I used my hip to close the refrigerator door. Then I set the items down on the counter beside the stove, barely saving the preserves jar from tipping onto the floor. "Trey, I predict that within six months you're gonna want to duct tape that mouth of hers."

"I doubt that very seriously. Her mouth is much too talented to tape up." The self-proclaimed geeky gamer wouldn't have dared to say something so sexually charged a few months ago, but then I knew from experience that Layla could be a potent testosterone booster.

Braden surged around the corner and into the kitchen, pulling a wrinkled t-shirt on over his head. His eyes were still foggy from sleep, his hair a disheveled mass of whorls and spikes. "What the hell, Atwood?"

I held up my hands in mock terror. "Whatever it is, I didn't do it."

"Yes, you did." He came to stand in front of me, looking genuinely angry. "You held out on me. I've been a fan of MMA for years, bought every pay-per-view, and gone to every live event I could. In all that time, the closest I've gotten to meeting any of the fighters is when they're doing fan selfies in the crowd. Then you come along with your *I Hate MMA*, and *MMA is not a real sport*. And suddenly you've got fighters coming to visit you? Sparring with you in the living room? Not to mention you've dated a supermodel. I don't get it. I would sell my soul to the devil to hang out with MMA fighters, and it just falls right into your lap. What have you done to deserve all of that? You don't even appreciate it."

Layla laughed and sat down at the table, pulling her legs up and hugging her knees to her chest. "Jamie actually did sell his soul to the devil."

I leaned around Braden to glare at her, bristling at her self-satisfied smile. Braden ignored us and kept right on with his inquiry.

"Why was he here in the first place? Last I heard, he was going out with your model. Now all of a sudden you guys are best friends?"

"Guess so. You want some eggs and bacon?" I indicated the food on the counter behind me. "Oh, dammit, I forgot the biscuits." I pushed past him and rummaged through the refrigerator until I found a can. Then I shoved past him again to preheat the oven and drag a cookie sheet out of the cabinet. "Could you put the biscuits on this pan for me, Braden? I need to get the eggs and bacon started."

Braden took the pan and the biscuits reluctantly over to the table, and Layla screamed when he slammed the can to pop it open. I turned my attention to the stove, melting butter in one pan before breaking eggs into it, then laying out bacon strips in the other. As I washed my hands in the sink, realizing too late that I was probably burning Kage again, I tried to figure out how I was going to explain the situation to my friends. Nothing I came up with seemed quite plausible.

"Hey, Jamie, I have a question." Layla sounded innocent, but I knew better. "Your fighter friend didn't seem too thrilled with Cameron. Why is that?"

My shoulders sagged as I turned to face her. "That's enough, Layla. This is not a fucking joke. This is people's lives."

I didn't mind her fucking with me. In fact, it seemed she and I had settled into a new groove of giving each other verbal hell, and I kind of enjoyed it. Sort of like a sibling rivalry. But, like my actual sister, Layla needed to realize that her teasing words had the potential to hurt.

"Whatever." She grabbed a raw biscuit, picking tiny pieces of dough off with her fingertips and popping them into her mouth. She took the hint, though, and was appropriately chastened if the subtle flush of her cheeks and the way she failed to make eye contact with anyone was any indication.

"Give me those biscuits before you eat them all." I snatched the pan from her and slid it into the hot oven. Then I flipped the scrambled eggs and turned the bacon, jumping when a bit of grease popped out onto my forearm.

Braden picked up where Layla left off. "Why can't we ask questions about what goes on in our own house? It's not like we're gonna go around telling Michael Kage's business. We can be discreet."

Great. He's not going to give up.

I turned and faced them all, letting out a big sigh, hoping they'd get the idea that I was at the end of my patience with them. "Look, guys, I realize you're all starving for drama, and my new friends and I are the closest thing you've got to that right now. But trust me when I say there is really no excitement here. Kage and Cameron are just new friends of mine. Hell, I don't even know them all that well yet. As for the almost-fight last night, whatever bad blood there is between them is their business. I just didn't want them fighting here and messing up our condo, that's all. Now stop with all of the questions."

God, what a web of lies I was weaving. If the truth ever did come out, I was going to look like an ass. Why had I ever told them I was dating Vanessa? That one detail was really screwing everything up. Otherwise, I could have just admitted that I'd interned for Kage over the summer. No big deal.

"Okay," Braden said. "I'll quit giving you the third degree if you'll get Kage to sign something for me next time you see him."

Yes! Now there was something I could work with.

"You can ask him yourself when he gets out of the shower. There can't be much hot water left, so it shouldn't be long."

Braden blinked. "He's here? In your shower? Are you telling me the Machine actually spent the night in our house?"

"Yes, the Machine actually spent the night in our house." I caught myself sporting a goofy grin and realized I was letting pride get in the way of logic. If I wasn't careful, Braden and the others would eventually figure out what was going on, and that was the last thing Kage needed. I had to give the impression that our relationship was casual. And new. "I told him he could crash here. No sense paying for a hotel room for just a few hours, right?" I avoided looking at Layla, who knew I was lying through my teeth.

Trey laughed at Braden, who was staring all moony-eyed in the direction of the bathroom. "Damn, Braden. I've never seen you so starstruck. Are you gonna be okay?"

"Don't tell me you wouldn't be the same way if Harley Quinn showed up right now. You would lose your shit."

"Um, yeah... But Harley Quinn is a female, not to mention a comic character. If she was walking around, that would mean that the laws of physics— of everything we know— had been altered. How can an MMA fighter showering in your house compare to that?"

Braden gave him a deadpan look, smacking his lips deliberately. "You really thought that one out, huh?"

"Hey, I can't help it if I'm logical. You were talking about a comic character coming to life. I would have to suspend a hell of a lot of disbelief in order to have that conversation with you."

"Who's Harley Quinn?" Layla asked.

Braden gladly took the opportunity to sell Trey down the river. "She's the Joker's girlfriend in the Batman comics, and Trey has a thing for her."

"That's an exaggeration." Trey squirmed and looked over at Layla. Then he added quietly, "She started out on *Batman: The Animated Series*, not the comics."

"Oh." Layla gave him one of her effortless flirty looks. "Do you want me to be Harley Quinn for Halloween?"

"Would you?" Trey's apprehension melted away. He glanced at her breasts, clearly already imagining her decked out in one of those barely there costumes that had transformed Halloween from a kid's holiday into an annual stripper convention. "Maybe we could celebrate early this year."

She giggled. "Sounds good to me. We can order costumes online. Are you going to be the Joker?"

"Hell, no. I'm going to be myself."

I laughed and dumped the scrambled eggs into a large serving bowl, then lined a plate with paper towels for the bacon. "You've just made his deepest fantasies come true," I called to Layla over my shoulder.

"Whose fantasies?" a deep voice asked from behind me, and I whirled around to find that Kage had finally emerged from the shower. His hair was wet, and one of my white t-shirts was stretched over his muscled body like a second skin, darkening in places where the water was seeping through. He'd also found a pair of sweatpants that were too large for me. They almost fit him, but I couldn't help noticing that he didn't appear to be wearing any underwear.

I gulped. "Hey."

"Hey," he returned, with a smile and a quick pass of his hand over his wet hair.

Braden stood up, nearly knocking over his chair in the process. "Michael! I mean, Mr. Kage! Could you sign something for me?" He grabbed the roll of paper towels from the table and shoved it toward Kage, who stared at him with an amused look on his face.

"I don't have a pen on me." Kage pretended to pat himself down, but there was most assuredly nowhere for a pen to hide under those tight clothes.

"You could always use blood," Layla suggested.

Kage smiled in her direction. "Are you donating? I'm pretty good at extracting it."

"So I've seen."

Sensing the impending showdown between my lover and my ex, and knowing that backing down was neither one's strong suit, I did the only thing I could think of. I grabbed the spatula and banged it on the side of the egg bowl. Then suddenly everyone was staring expectantly at me, so I figured I probably ought to come up with something to say.

"Uh... I cooked breakfast." I aimed the comment toward Kage, but that didn't stop the others from giving me matching looks that clearly said, *No shit.*

Kage's flinty stare, left over from his near-altercation with Layla, softened as he regarded me standing there holding the spatula. His eyes crinkled slightly at the corners, and his lips tightened down on the affectionate smile that threatened to escape. I cursed my own reaction— the fine tremor in my fingers, and the way my breath caught in my throat. This was bad. I mean really bad. If my friends witnessed the effect he had on me, especially without the fog of alcohol to disguise it, they'd be onto us within minutes.

Kage took a step toward me and craned his neck to peer over my shoulder. "You've been holding out on me, James. I had no idea you were so domestic."

I spun around, putting my back squarely to him while I struggled to think up a suitable comeback.

"He's not domestic," Trey said. "He never cooks."

Silently thanking Trey for throwing me under the bus, I resisted the urge to tell Layla that her new boyfriend had only recently become acquainted with our washing machine and dryer. *The things we did for love.* Trey had cleaned up to get Layla, I had cooked to impress Kage, and he would choke down the greasy eggs and bacon to please me. Or at least I hoped he would.

"I have cooked plenty of times." I grabbed the eggs and bacon and headed over to the table just as the oven timer started beeping to announce the biscuits were done. I turned back, getting flustered that things seemed to be happening so fast, and now everyone was going to be thinking about how I was cooking just because I had company. Did people cook for their buddies, treat their visit like a special occasion? I know I never had. And now here I was acting like my mom, dragging out the food and trying to entertain.

Sensing my anxiety, Kage held up a hand to me. "I'll get the biscuits. You just put those on the table." He picked up the hot pads from the counter and pulled the biscuits from the oven, setting them on the wire cooling rack next to the stove. Then he turned to me. "Where are the plates and utensils?"

Braden jumped up and opened the cabinet that held our mismatched plates, apparently interested in lending a hand now that Kage was the one he'd be helping. "You get those, I'll get the silverware. I already got the paper towels, which you never signed, by the way. You don't really have to use blood. I have a sharpie somewhere around here."

Kage laughed as he grabbed a stack of plates. "Just chill, man. I'll sign something better than a paper towel for you."

"Sorry, I was just worried you'd leave before I got something."

"I'll be in town for a while, so no worries."

"You will?" I blurted. "Are you sure that's a good idea? I mean, how long? Won't your uncle…" I trailed off, unsure of exactly what my objection was to Kage hanging around for a while. We weren't any more conspicuous as a couple in Georgia than we were in Nevada.

"You want me to go?" The wounded tone of his voice cut deep, and I immediately thought of our visit to my parents' house. No way were we going to have a replay of that.

"Hell, no," I told him resolutely. "Of course not. I was just thinking about your situation, that's all. We haven't really discussed it in detail." I raised my eyebrows at him— a not-too-subtle hint that there were things that probably needed to be succinctly spelled out, but not right now, and not in front of my friends.

His stern expression challenged me, nearly forced me to look away. "I think we've said all that needs to be said on the subject. At this point, we're just talking in circles."

"What do your PR people say?"

"I don't answer to them. I'm the boss. I pay their fucking salaries."

The raw anger in his voice stunned me, and all I could do was sit down and start absently serving my breakfast. I barely even registered what I was putting on the plate.

"You gonna eat all the eggs?" Trey asked.

"Sorry." I glanced down at the heaping pile of eggs and started scraping them back into the bowl. Kage crossed the room and leaned against the counter. The borrowed t-shirt rode too high in that position, skimming just above his belly button and exposing a strip of tan flesh that had me distracted, salivating.

Trey started laughing. "Jeez, Jamie. Make up your mind. Do you want all of the eggs, or none?"

I looked down and discovered that I'd scraped every bit of egg back into the serving bowl. "Oh, forget it." I slammed my empty plate down on the table and folded my arms across my chest. "Y'all just eat. I'm not hungry anymore."

"You don't need bacon anyway," Kage pointed out. "And definitely not those biscuits. You still need to watch what you eat, even when I can't be around to help."

"Yes, daddy," I said, bitterness making my voice tight. "Do you know how ridiculous you look trying to be all bossy while wearing my clothes that are too small for you? That shirt is practically a cutoff."

"Yeah?" Suddenly the edge was gone from his demeanor, and his tone was playful. "You don't think I look authoritative enough in your shirt? How about this?" He pulled it up over his head, balled it up, and threw it at me. I caught it without thinking, because all I was conscious of was his bare chest and abdomen, and the fact that we were standing in the kitchen with my friends looking on. I wanted to cover him with a dish towel or something.

He stalked toward me with a cocky swagger that had my knees melting, backing me into a corner formed by the edge of the refrigerator and the wall. "Can I be your daddy now?" he asked, resting his hand on the wall behind my head and leaning in.

I stared at him, swallowing around the dry piece of wood that was my tongue, feeling it catch in my throat. His dick was within inches of mine, and I could smell the soap on his skin and feel his breath against my cheek. I tried not to make eye contact with him, but I couldn't ignore the proximity of his body. He knew it, too; the lecherous grin on his face was proof of that. He was purposely goading me, and I wasn't sure what to do about it. My head was a swirl of confusion, and my cock was hard. I was within seconds of saying fuck it and wrapping my legs around his waist. I wanted to feel his steely length pressing against me through the fabric of those dangerously revealing sweat pants.

Instead, I ducked beneath his arm and escaped, stuttering unintelligibly. I needed to do something to wipe that look of stunned confusion off of my friends' faces. Even Layla looked shocked, because knowing Kage and I were lovers and seeing him flaunting it in front of my roommates were two entirely different things.

I laughed nervously and addressed my friends. "He loves to kid around. A side effect of being the most aggressive, testosterone-overloaded male on the planet." I held up the wadded t-shirt. "I'm going to go find a shirt that fits him better. Can't have him cruising around here shirtless and putting the rest of us to shame."

I didn't look back at Kage. I hoped he would follow me so we could have a powwow in the bedroom, but he didn't. I rummaged through my drawers and closets for ten minutes, and all I could find was a dark blue Nike t-shirt our basketball coach had passed out to the team the previous year. Everyone knew I liked my t-shirts tight, but I'd received a size large instead of my usual medium, so I'd shoved the thing into the bottom drawer. I cursed the suggestive slogan written across the front in neon yellow, knowing I had no choice but to give it to him, and hurried back to the kitchen with it clutched in my hand. Fortunately my dick had calmed down during the search, so at least that was one thing I didn't have to be embarrassed about.

When I returned, Kage was leaning on the counter as if nothing unusual had just happened. He and Braden were engaged in a heated discussion about which was the better discipline for MMA, grappling or striking. My friends were making quick work of the food I'd cooked, but that was okay with me. The events of the morning had effectively demolished my appetite for food.

I tossed Kage the t-shirt, and he pulled it over his head while continuing to talk to Braden. Fortunately the length of it covered most of his commando crotch. He glanced absently down at the front of the shirt as he attempted to smooth out the wrinkles, but then he caught sight of the slogan: *Skilled in Every Position.*

He cocked an eyebrow at me. "You trying to tell me something?"

My face burned red. "It's a basketball thing." I turned away and moved to the opposite side of the room, trying not to think about the night before and how Kage had proved for the first time that he was indeed skilled in every position.

Braden, oblivious to our volley of innuendo, continued pleading his case to Kage. "I was always under the impression that wrestling was the best base training. So many wrestlers become MMA fighters, and it seems like most fights eventually go to the ground. Maybe not in the Heavyweight Division, but in the others. You're in Welterweight, and those guys spend a lot of time on the ground."

Kage nodded. "There's some truth to that, but I think it's more important to be able to stand and bang. In most instances, a great fighter can avoid being taken down simply by keeping out of the clinch or by sprawling effectively, which makes a good ground game secondary. Against most opponents, I can keep my distance, get in and out, and do a shitload of damage with my punches and kicks. There are plenty of talented fighters who focus on their ground game, but I think knockout power and striking accuracy are two of my most important assets in the octagon."

"That's easy for you to say," Braden continued. "You have an amazing ground game, too. You're such a technical fighter, even in your submission attempts. So deliberate and calculating. What about those guys who have almost no ground game? Let somebody shoot their legs and then lay on them for four minutes, and they're toast."

"I see you've been paying attention," Kage said appreciatively. "I've only had two UFC fights, and you've picked up a lot about how I work."

"Dude, I know my shit when it comes to MMA. And you only have to see a world-class fighter dominate the octagon one time to know. You don't flail or second-guess, and there's no doubt in your face, even when you get tagged. But can I just say that it scared the shit out of me when you started taunting Diaz last night? I wish you wouldn't do that. It has the potential to turn ugly. Just look at Weidman vs. Silva if you don't believe me. Silva was fucking around and taunting Weidman, and then *Bam*! K.O. Bye-bye belt."

Kage chuckled, but I could see the darkness lurking behind his eyes.

"Kage won't ever stop doing that." My own voice surprised me. I hadn't meant to join in on the conversation.

"Well, he should," Braden said. "It's not smart."

"He can't stop. It's part of who he is." I held Kage's gaze as I replied to Braden. "If you knew him better, you wouldn't be worried, though. He knows what he's doing. Nothing he does is ever accidental."

3

(KAGE)

THE CONVERSATION DIED in the kitchen as Jamie's roommates and Layla-the-jealous-bitch continued to pick over the food on the table. Jamie just stood near the refrigerator watching them with a blank expression on his face.

"Come on, Jamie. Let's go get something cleaner to eat."

He blinked at me, as if unable to comprehend my words. "You don't want any of the food I cooked?"

"Well, I love that you went to the trouble of cooking for me. It was nice. I just don't think there's enough for everyone." I looked pointedly at his friends scarfing down the food. "Besides, I'd like to visit your school and see if it's anything like I've been imagining when I picture you in class."

"Oh, how sweet," Layla mumbled around a mouthful of bacon.

I figured Jamie might prefer it if I ignored her, but I didn't. "Could you swallow that mouthful of fat before you speak? It's not very attractive."

Trey stopped chewing and stared at me, and I knew what he was thinking. He was thinking, *Man, I'd love to come to my girl's defense... But then he'd probably kick my ass.* Or something to that effect. He was smarter than he was brave, so he kept his mouth shut.

Jamie, however, wasn't afraid of me.

"Kage, could you please not?"

"Please not what?" I demanded, moving to stand directly in front of him. "She started it. Am I just supposed to ignore her obvious digs? Dammit, you know what she's doing. She might as well come right out and call us—"

Jamie slapped a hand over my mouth. I swear to God, if it had been anyone else pulling that shit, they would have been picking themselves up off the floor. As it was, I grabbed him roughly by the wrist and snatched his hand from my lips, squeezing his arm. I saw him wince, so I eased up on my grip.

"Don't fucking cover my mouth, Jamie." I took a deep breath and closed my eyes, working hard to stay calm. Then I released his arm. "Let's just go, okay? I'm getting hungry."

He nodded, and no one tried to speak to us as we left the kitchen. Jamie grabbed his car keys off his bedside table, and then he reached out to unplug his phone from the charger. I shushed him with a finger against my lips and depressed the device's power switch. Then I removed it from the charger and placed my own phone beside it on the table.

"What if we have an emergency?" he asked.

"It'll be fine. Just be quiet for a minute."

He looked skeptical, but he did as I asked and left his phone without a word. Once we were outside, I pulled Jamie into an alcove near his condo door and explained.

"Remember I told you I thought our phones were being blocked and possibly tapped?"

He nodded, his forehead wrinkling in alarm.

"Well, I got to thinking… Aaron is paranoid as hell, and he's always imagining somebody's watching or listening to him, so that's nothing new. But he happens to be a surveillance expert, and he said that anyone can use your phone as a listening device, like a bug. All they have to do is access your phone while it's hooked in to a network, and they can either infiltrate one of your installed apps or do a stealth install of a new app."

"Are you for real? That sounds like something from a James Bond movie. Also, I thought Aaron was mute."

"Nah, he can talk just fine. But he only talks around people he trusts. Probably a side effect of working in surveillance. I imagine that knowing all of the ways someone could be listening to you might make you scared to say anything important or incriminating unless you feel completely safe. Anyway, Aaron said the way to tell if your phone has been compromised is to charge it to a hundred percent, power it down, and then leave it off of the charger for several hours. A phone that's being used as a bug will function even with the power off, which means the battery will still run down."

"Uh…" Jamie ran a hand through his hair and whipped his head around, presumably looking for spies. "That is really creepy. Why would someone be using my phone as a listening device?"

"It's all about me. You know that."

"But why? I don't understand. This isn't a movie, Kage."

I went to shove my hands into my pockets, only to discover I was wearing Jamie's ridiculous sweatpants, so I fiddled with the string instead. It was so difficult to be completely honest with him. Not because I didn't want to share, but because I worried about him. Maybe knowing too much wasn't a good thing for a clueless college boy who was flirting with the dark side.

"My uncle is used to getting his way, that's all. He knows how I feel about you, and he doesn't like it."

"So what does that mean exactly? That he's tapping my phone? That he's bugging me? That he's watching me?"

"Well, he's definitely blocked our calls to each other and listened in on conversations. That I know for sure. The other stuff has yet to be proven. I just…"

"You just what?" he prompted.

"I was thinking about a lot of things while I was in the shower. About the phone call blocks, and the fact that my uncle has gotten personal information about you since you left Vegas. He had pictures of you and that asshole Cameron outside your condo, and inside— taken through your bedroom window." Jamie looked horrified, but the stuff I'd been keeping to myself had already started to bubble out, and I couldn't slow down. Damage control would have to wait until later. "The fact that, while I was in the limo, Aaron just happened to be telling Aldo how to tell if a phone has been tampered with… and then you said someone sent you a video of us together in my apartment. I don't know, I'm trying to work it all out. The person who sent you the video didn't threaten you or ask for anything?"

"No. They just sent me an anonymous text with no return number. It came in while I was in my room with Cameron, after he kissed me." His voice was shaky, his eyes concerned. He was afraid, and I hated that I was the cause of it. But that didn't stop me from being pissed.

I grated, "So you were about to fuck Cameron—"

"No! I wasn't. But you have to understand, it was confusing not knowing if you were done with me. You wouldn't answer my calls, but I still told Cameron I had a boyfriend. He thought I was crazy being faithful to a guy who was so obviously ignoring me, but I just couldn't move on if there was a chance with you. That's the honest-to-god truth."

I took a deep, shuddering breath. Inside, I was cursing the situation. Cursing myself for not putting the puzzle pieces together sooner, and for letting affection and insecurity blind me to some pretty obvious shit that was going on around me. Hell, I was as bad as Jamie. I'd repeatedly accused him of being clueless and naïve, and all the while my uncle and his goons had been circling us and slowly tightening the perimeter. Now I'd been manipulated into presenting a media persona that wasn't me, and Jamie's life was being threatened. He may not have known what it all meant, but I did.

My uncle's plan was for me to marry Vanessa and become an MMA Champion. Jamie was an unfortunate bump in the road that would eventually be smoothed out. I had no idea how far my uncle would go to get his way in the matter. If he would sabotage Jamie's college or professional career, buy him off with an offer he couldn't refuse, manipulate one or both of us into betraying the other in some way. The possibilities were endless. I'd tried to keep Jamie out of things— out of my uncle's way— but I hadn't done a good enough job. I had underestimated the seriousness of the situation, believing that if we just flew under his radar for a while, he'd lose interest. Now things were serious.

But I couldn't think about all of that until I was back in Vegas, away from Jamie so that I could think clearly. It was as if he gave off some sort of signal that interfered with my brain waves, like when you get anything wireless too close to a microwave.

I would protect him, though, at any cost. There was no way my uncle was going to get away with ruining Jamie's life. These days, he was all I cared about.

"Okay, listen up." I looked him squarely in the eyes, trying to convey a sense of confidence that I only partially felt. "We're going to go get new phones. That's the first order of business. Whether they're wires or just being blocked and intercepted, we need new ones anyway. We'll get burner phones so they can't be tracked, but we'll still keep our old phones so that it's not obvious. Only use our old phones for stuff we don't mind being overheard or recorded, just as a cover so they don't realize we're onto them. Just to buy us some time until I can figure out what to do."

There was a fine tremor in his hand as he ran it through his hair. "I'm scared, Kage. This all sounds so… How should I act? I don't know how to deal with shit like this. What are they going to do to me?"

Guilt washed over me again. Not only was I putting Jamie in a precarious position, but I was also terrifying him. I grabbed him and pulled him into a hug. "Don't worry about a thing. I guess I should have told you up front that there's no real danger here. No physical danger, anyway. It's just my uncle playing his head games. He's trying to break us up, that's all, and any information he can get that will make that happen is what he's after. If he can find some dirt on you, he will. If he can put doubt in our heads, he will. That's why he showed me the photos of you and Cameron. He wanted me to believe you had been unfaithful, so that I would break up with you."

"But you didn't," he murmured against my chest.

"No, baby. I didn't. I came and got your ass." I dropped a kiss onto the top of his head. "Look… think of my uncle and his goons as overzealous paparazzi. That's all they are. They're just looking for dirt to use against us, while also making sure that the press doesn't get a hold of any real dirt. Does that make sense?"

He nodded.

"Don't worry about your safety," I added. "But do worry about your privacy."

"Okay."

"In the meantime, we have a lot to do. New phones, new clothes for me, some food, and a tour of the school. And when you get your new phone, I want you to call your mom and tell her we'll be stopping by tomorrow after you get out of class."

Jamie looked skeptical as he untangled himself from our embrace and led me out to the parking lot. When he stopped at an old BMW and climbed inside, I frowned.

"This is your car?" I slid into the passenger seat, feeling the seat shift on its unsteady base. The dashboard was cracked, and I noticed that the back window of the convertible top was taped in place.

"It's a loaner. My real car is in the shop. "

"Really?" I was so relieved to know that he didn't have to drive around every day in that death trap. "Can we pick your car up today?"

Jamie's laugh was weak— his embarrassed laugh. "I was kidding, Kage. This is my car."

"Oh." I ran my hand along the cracked dashboard and took in the state of the buttons on the electronics panel. Most of the labels were rubbed off of the buttons. "Sorry, I didn't mean to be rude. It's just... Let's go get you a new car."

Jamie stomped on the brake before he'd even gotten all the way out of the parking lot. "Are you insane? You can't just buy me a car."

"Why not?"

He looked confused. "I don't know. You just can't."

I raised my brows and crossed my arms over my chest. "Give me one good reason why I can't. And it has to be a logical reason."

"I don't know. You remember what my dad said about you buying me."

"Are we really going to go there again? Jamie, I can buy things for you, and you can let me fuck you, and it's all okay. What does your dad think is going to happen if I spend money on you? That you're going to end up on the streets selling your body for drugs?"

"Maybe." He laughed. "But couldn't you come up with a less seedy whore fantasy for me? I'd rather imagine myself with some rich guy who supports me in exchange for sex. He'd stop by my rent-paid luxury apartment a couple of times a week to use my body."

"So you're sticking with guys, huh?" I teased.

"What do you mean?"

"They were your words, not mine. You said 'I'd rather imagine myself with some rich guy...'"

"Hmmm. I did, didn't I?" His lips stretched into a crooked smile, and he glanced away. "Guess you've spoiled me."

"Spoiling you is what I'm *trying* to do, but you won't let me. Quit being stubborn and tell me what kind of car you want. I need to do this for you. This car is not safe, and it's really ugly. Not to mention it smells like an old gym sock filled with buttered popcorn."

"Your uncle won't like it if you buy me a car."

"What can he do about it? He can't take it, because it's going to be in your name. That would be stealing."

"Kage..."

"How about a Range Rover?"

"Yes," he blurted, clearly as surprised at his answer as I was. "I mean no. That's ridiculous. Those things are expensive just for the sake of being expensive."

"Are they? You went so crazy over the limo that Aldo and Aaron drive us around in. That's why I thought of it. Of course, we'd get you a sporty one instead of the long wheel base."

"Kage, I'm a used BMW kind of guy. I wouldn't look right in a nice ride."

"I can easily see you in a Range Rover. And you looked really hot driving my Vette. I would have suggested one of those, but we really need something with more than two seats, and a cargo area for hauling stuff around, don't you think? Who knows where we may need to go now that I'm in the UFC and you're about to graduate. And what if we just want to pack up and take a vacation? Drive up the coast or something, or take a bed and breakfast tour. We need an SUV."

"It would be for both of us, then?" His face said he was considering it now.

"Yeah. Only you'd sort of keep it."

"In that case, I guess I can't say no. I already feel bad for making you ride around in this broken-down hunk of garbage." Jamie pulled out onto the road with a reserved sigh.

"Damn, I've never heard anyone so depressed about getting a new car. This is a good thing, okay? I don't like the idea of you riding around in something that could leave you on the side of the road, or worse." I frowned and glanced suspiciously around the car. "This isn't about being sentimental, is it? You worried about losing the stains on the backseat from where you and the Mexi-bitch had sex?"

He rolled his eyes at me. "I don't have the slightest clue who you're talking about. Did I ever date a Mexi-bitch? I can't seem to remember."

Jamie knew the way to the Land Rover dealership, but we needed to take care of our other business first, starting with food. The restaurant Jamie chose was decent. For a healthy eatery, there were some questionable items on the menu, including several sugary desserts that made me shake my head. But it was fun eating together after weeks apart. Jamie was the only person who could make me see eating as anything besides a necessary function for survival.

"What are you smiling about," Jamie asked, jogging me out of my thoughts.

"Just remembering your birthday meal, and that bucket of vanilla root beer I chugged."

Jamie laughed. "Yeah, and those greasy bacon burgers."

"And the white cake at Enzo's."

"Our wedding cake," Jamie mused. "I miss Enzo. I miss everything... Mostly you."

For some reason, that made me feel a blush coming on. I took another bite of food as a distraction, and the rest of the meal took on a pensive tone.

During our shopping spree to get our burner phones, it did occur to me that if someone was following us, then keeping our old phones wouldn't be an effective sleight of hand. But then, who cared if we were being followed? They couldn't actually do anything to us, so we might as well enjoy ourselves. Jamie seemed to have been swayed by my efforts to convince him that there was no real danger, and that was a very good thing.

Our dealership visit went awkward the minute we stepped onto the showroom floor and every eye zeroed in on me. I wish I could say it was because of my staggering good looks, or because I was a recognized celebrity now, or even because I had the most adorable guy in the world at my side. But none of those things were the reason I'd drawn everyone's attention.

"Why didn't you remind me to go get clothes first?" I mumbled at Jamie out of the side of my mouth as the first salesman approached. "I look like a jackass."

The rail-thin sales manager who sashayed over to us made no secret of looking down his nose at me and my shirt. "Skilled in every position. How charming." As his eyes ate up every inch of me, I was certain of two things: He thought there was no way in hell I could afford one of his precious cars, and he wanted to suck my dick. Let's just say it was a pleasure shutting him down on both counts.

We chose a black Range Rover Autobiography with a navy blue and gray interior. Top of the line. Fuck you, buddy.

"Jesus Christ, Kage." Jamie pulled me aside and gaped when the salesman stepped away to get our paperwork started, leaving us standing beside the vehicle we'd claimed as our own. "You can't spend almost two hundred grand on a car. We could buy my dream house with that."

"Jamie, that's not a dream house. It's just a house. You deserve better."

"No, I don't. What are you doing?" He glanced toward the dealership office, then back at my determined face. "You're doing it because of him, aren't you? Because he teased you about your shirt."

"Of course not. And he didn't just tease me about my shirt. He insinuated that I couldn't afford to buy you one of these things. Fuck him. I can buy you whatever you want. Tell me something you want, and we'll go buy it right now."

Jamie stifled a laugh, and I'll admit it infuriated me just a little bit. "I've never seen you like this. It's cute."

I just glared at him.

"Are you sure you have the money for this?"

"What do you think?" I asked, still glaring.

"All right, I'm in. Just to defend your honor, I will accept a car that costs four times what most people make in a year. What else can I do to help? Act stuck-up?"

His playfulness finally coaxed a smile to my face. "He wants me, you know. He's been raping me with his beady little eyes ever since we got here. Don't you wanna do something about that?"

"Maybe." His wicked smile had me thinking maybe I was in for a treat. And when the salesman returned, Jamie did not disappoint.

He stood directly in front of me, wrapped his arms around my waist, and plastered his body to mine. The pose was aggressively intimate, and I loved it. "Sir, before we pay for this thing, we were wondering one more thing."

"What's that?" The man frowned, clearly annoyed at our public display of affection, but Jamie wasn't finished yet. Not by a long shot. In addition to being downright gorgeous, my man can seduce like a pro without even trying. It just comes naturally for him, and most of the time he doesn't even notice the effect he has on people. I've seen it enough to know. In the case of the obnoxious car salesman, I predicted Jamie was going to poke out that suckable bottom lip and turn on the sweet little twink routine that I was convinced could inspire dirty thoughts in any red blooded man's head, gay or straight. He did that and so much more.

He flashed that head-down, eyes-up puppy dog pout that always got him whatever he wanted. "Could you show us one more time how the back seats lie down? We're not sure if everything is going to fit back there."

The man opened the back of the SUV and demonstrated. When the seats had retracted into the floor, Jamie crawled up into the back on his hands and knees. I climbed in after him, sensing exactly where this was going and loving it. Jamie turned onto his back, and without needing a prompt, I nudged my body up between his legs.

"Oh, yeah," he said, his voice far too suggestive for a business transaction. He twined them around my waist and hooked his ankles together, taking things a little too far when he rubbed his crotch against my barely contained dick. "Oh, yeah," he groaned. "God, yes, that's a perfect fit. What do you think, baby?"

"I think I should have worn underwear," I said where only he could hear, reaching down to adjust myself. Then I called over my shoulder to the salesman. "We'll take it."

After that, the salesman couldn't get us off of the lot fast enough. They gave us a few bucks for Jamie's beat-up car, and I called my banker in Vegas and had him handle the details. All told, the process took less than two hours, and I drove away feeling I'd been vindicated.

Jamie asked me to drive, since he wasn't familiar with driving such a large vehicle. "I'd be fine on the interstate, but I need a little practice with it before I try to battle Atlanta traffic." I didn't bother telling him I'd never driven an SUV, either. Not to mention it would be my first time in Atlanta traffic. It gave me a sense of pride to know that he considered me capable enough to handle the things he couldn't, and I wasn't about to blow his image of me. I'd succeed or die trying.

He was quiet for a while as I familiarized myself with the flow of traffic. Then he tensed and spun in his seat. "What if someone back there recognized you? After that thing we did in the back with the seats? God, I'm such an idiot."

"It'll be fine," I told him.

"But he could have known who you were all along. Or someone else there might have known. What if they—"

"I'm tired of what if. Just tell me how to get to the school." Weariness crept into my voice, because I really did not want to have this conversation anymore.

Jamie brightened. "You were serious about visiting the campus? I thought you were just making excuses to get out of the condo."

"No, I was being honest. You should try it sometime." And there it was again. If I didn't want to have the conversation, why did I keep bringing it up?

He whipped his head around and fixed me with a wounded-dog look. "I'm honest."

"With your friends?"

"It's complicated." He stared out the window. "And the secrecy is more for you than me. I've told you that a million times."

"How selfless of you. I must have gotten the wrong idea. Maybe because just a little while ago, you were frotting with me in front of a car salesman who might very well have recognized me. Where was the concern then? I realize that you are legitimately worried about what might happen to me if the media found out about us. But can you admit that at least some of it has nothing to do with my career?"

"Yes, okay? Are you happy? I admit I have some lingering feelings of... doubt. I don't know what people will think, or how my friends will take the news. But I'm going to tell them, because whether you believe it or not, I do want them to know. The question is, are you actually going to be okay with the results? What if there's blowback? How are you gonna feel when one of my friends lets it slip to the wrong person, and then the press finds out? Are you really willing to risk your contract— everything you've worked for— just to have the satisfaction of knowing I'm not ashamed of you?"

"You're goddamn right I am. If you haven't figured that out yet, you're not as smart as I thought you were."

"Well, do it then," he yelled. "*Fuck!* I'm done trying to protect you. Like you told Steve, you're a grown man. You can make your own decisions. I don't care who knows. Tell them all. Fucking announce it in the octagon in your next post-fight interview for all I care. Just... don't blame me if it goes bad."

"I don't need you to protect me," I said.

We were silent for a while as I threaded the Rover through a sea of vehicles. Jamie kept his eyes trained on the spot right outside his window, and I squeezed the steering wheel and stewed over his words, wondering if he'd really meant them. If he was really giving me unconditional permission to come out and take him with me. Because if that's what he was doing, shit was about to get real.

There were a lot of SUV's on the road. I'd never noticed how many until I was driving one myself. It seemed a large percentage of them were Escalades, with a smattering of random other brands peppered in, while I had yet to spot another Rover.

After a while, traffic slowed and then came to a stop. "You think there's an accident ahead?" I asked Jamie.

"No telling." He didn't look at me, and his voice was flat. "You'll learn soon enough, traffic in this town is either Autobahn fast, or it's standing still." After a couple of minutes, movement in my peripheral vision caught my eye, and I turned to see Jamie having what looked like a sign language conversation with the guy in the Escalade next to us.

My first thought was that one of us had a flat tire or an open gas compartment door, but soon it became clear that the man was trying to flirt with Jamie. He held his cell phone against the glass, and I could see that he'd used the handwriting feature to scrawl out his number on the screen in red.

"What the fuck... Is that guy trying to give you his number?"

"Uh... yeah." Jamie looked terrified. "I was trying to tell him politely that I wasn't interested."

"Politely?" I leaned across Jamie's lap and held my middle finger up to the glass of the passenger window. The guy gave me the finger right back, and I *almost* liked him for it. "There. Message delivered."

Apparently my comment amused Jamie. "Real classy, babe. Want me to moon him?"

"No, he'd love that." I settled back into the driver's seat as traffic rolled a few feet and then stopped again. I cut my eyes over at the creep, who was still beside us.

"Ooh, I think somebody's jealous." Jamie cocked an eyebrow at me and bit his lip, flirting deliberately with me. I tried to ignore the way my heart sped up.

"Not jealous. I just want to make sure other drivers adhere to the rules of etiquette. It's bad manners to try to hook up in traffic."

Jamie chuckled and placed a hand on my thigh, running his fingers down between my legs and grazing my balls through the sweatpants. "How about a blow job? Is that poor traffic etiquette?"

"Actually, it's the politest thing you can do in traffic."

He lowered the band of the sweats and pulled out my stiffening erection. His fingers encircled my cock, and he tormented my sensitive flesh, dragging with light touches, driving me mad.

"Don't be a tease, Jamie. Get over here and suck it." I grabbed him by the back of the head, threading my fingers through his hair, and pulled him down toward my lap. Only he didn't give. Instead, he pulled against me, challenging me with an arrogant grin.

"Make me."

His words went straight to my dick. He was riling me up on purpose, drawing my dark needs out of their hiding place and into the daylight, right in the middle of downtown traffic. At that moment, I couldn't have wanted him more.

Keeping my hand wrapped around the back of his head, I used my strength to reel him in before I crushed my lips to his. The kiss was brutal and sloppy, with no pretense of romance. After I was done bruising his soft lips, I dragged my tongue along his jaw before angling down and latching onto the pulse point on the side of his throat. I bit into it and sucked hard, determined to leave the nastiest hickey possible, knowing he would be mortified to have to go home with the telltale mark. My heart surged at the warm softness and salty flavor of his skin in my mouth, and the feel of him squirming against me.

When I let go of him, his expression was panic stricken. He flipped down the visor to examine himself, running a finger lightly over the wicked purple mark just beneath his jaw.

"Look where you put that thing," he said accusingly. "There's no way I'll be able to hide it. Even a turtle neck wouldn't help."

I grinned and sat forward in my seat again, flipping the band of my pants back up to cover my throbbing erection. "That's what you get for challenging me. Now I don't want the blow job anymore. But tonight, I'm going to fuck you so hard, you might wish you had just chosen to shut up and suck my dick."

"You're a confusing bastard," he said. But a side glance revealed him touching the mark on his throat, his chest heaving with excitement.

4

(JAMIE)

AFTER I SHOWED Kage around the Georgia State campus, or at least the places that were significant to me, we headed back to the condo. We skipped the clothes shopping, deciding that Kage could handle another day in my clothes, and we'd stop by the mall on the way to my parents' house after class the next day. After the excitement and the arguing, we were both ready to get home and regroup. I was nervous about my friends finding out that I had a brand new vehicle in the parking lot, and even more apprehensive about the glaring mark on my throat. I mean, how in the hell was I going to explain leaving the house with Kage and coming back with a hickey?

We entered to the familiar sound of Braden and Trey trying to kill things on some video game.

"Finally, you guys are back!" Braden looked up long enough to acknowledge us, and then went back to pounding frantically on the controller, his tongue stuck out and his brows nearly touching in the center. Miranda lounged beside him with her legs stretched across his lap, reading one of her e-books. She watched us suspiciously as we crossed the room, as did Layla, who was curled up beside Trey like a lazy kitten, her blond head resting on his lap.

We popped into my room for a few minutes to check our phones. As Kage had suspected, the battery power had diminished on both devices.

He leaned down to speak close to my ear. "Do you have your important things backed up? Pictures, videos…"

I nodded.

"Then let's just forget about keeping these things around. Now that I know they're listening in, I just want to get as far away from them as possible. Is that okay with you?"

"Definitely."

Kage gathered them up and took them outside. He put them on the ground in the parking lot and ran over them with our new SUV, and then he dropped them in the trash can for the city to pick up.

When we entered the house for the second time, I felt lighter knowing that the phones were gone. Now we had our privacy back, or at least some of it.

I sat down in the comfy gray corduroy armchair Trey had brought from his parents' house, and Kage dropped down onto the floor in front of me, settling back into the space between my legs. He appeared relaxed, propping an arm up on my knee. I, on the other hand, was ramrod stiff, my neck canted at an odd angle to keep from displaying the aching love bite at my jaw. I considered asking Layla to put some makeup on it for me, but then I remembered how she'd treated Kage at breakfast. I didn't want to get a row started between them again, so I just kept quiet and prayed that my little problem would somehow go unnoticed.

The afternoon passed by in a haze of video games and meaningless chatter. The girls barely spoke to us, though I caught them staring at us often. My paranoia suggested that Layla had spilled our secret to Miranda. I had no proof, but Miranda had always been talkative around me before, and now she seemed awkward. I was glad when the girls finally got up to leave.

"Got a report due Monday," Miranda explained to Braden. "I haven't even started on it, so I'll be busy all day tomorrow."

"But I'm getting used to you staying over," Braden whined, setting down his game controller and grabbing her wrist as she tried to make her escape. "I won't know what to do without you sleeping in my bed until lunchtime tomorrow."

Braden sandwiched her cheeks between his palms and devoured her mouth in a kiss that probably should have been reserved for the bedroom. She leaned into it, and after a minute she was giggling quietly. "Okay, I'll try to stop by tomorrow. I know you can't go without it for twenty-four hours."

Braden growled and reached around to grab her ass. "Don't forget me."

"I won't," she promised. Then she looked over at me and Kage. "Bye, guys. Nice to meet you, Kage. We'll be watching you on fight nights."

Kage beamed at the attention, which was so cute and unlike him I almost laughed. "Thanks, Miranda. Nice meeting you, too. And good luck on your paper."

"Romantic Lit. Ugh." She rolled her eyes. "I thought it was going to be like romance novels, not this old-fashioned, wordy bullshit."

"I have to go, too," Layla said suddenly, jumping up from the sofa. "I don't want to be the only girl in this guy party."

Not to be outdone by Braden and Miranda's steamy goodbye, she leaned over Trey, giving me and Kage a clear view of her ass, and laid a sloppy kiss on him. The scene brought back a strong memory of her unique feminine scent and the way it felt to be on the receiving end of one of those kisses, and I felt guilty even thinking such a thing with Kage right there, touching me. I wanted to reach out and touch him back, to reassure him— no, to reassure me. Because I wasn't sure exactly what I was feeling. I hadn't felt even a twinge of attraction for Layla since I'd met Kage. While he wasn't around, everything had been strictly platonic between us. But now that I was sitting here watching my ex-girlfriend tongue fuck her new guy's mouth, not being able to do the same to my boyfriend, was maddening. It was as if the afternoon had turned into some couples battle, and Kage and I were the losers.

That's what it was, I realized. Layla was challenging me, and I felt helpless and needy. I longed to have that kind of relationship again— not with her, but one I could show off and be proud of.

I rested a hand on Kage's shoulder, and felt his muscles tense in response. Otherwise, neither one of us moved.

After the girls had finished one-upping each other's boyfriend game, they left, carrying the awkwardness with them. I hadn't realized how tense I was until then.

Seeming to sense how I felt, or possibly feeling the same himself, Kage shrugged his shoulders up and down. "Boy, I could sure use a rubdown. My muscles are really fucking sore after last night's fight."

"I'll do it," Braden blurted, rubbing his hands together. "I give a kick-ass sports massage, if I do say so myself."

Kage and I both froze, and nearly lost it when he looked at me over his shoulder and mouthed, "What the fuck?"

"Um…" I choked down a laugh. "Let me. I know how he likes it."

Kage glanced once more at me over his shoulder and stuck out his tongue in a suggestive way that made my asshole tighten as I imagined what he might have done with it if we'd been alone.

Braden frowned. "Okay, if Kage wants to pass on this expertise."

"Well, Jamie and I have known each other for a while," Kage explained to Braden. "We've gotten pretty familiar with each other. When he said he knows how I like it, he wasn't kidding. He knows pretty much everything there is to know about me."

I was impressed. Kage had not lied about anything.

Braden nodded dejectedly, and I couldn't help feeling sorry for him. He had no idea why he'd been shot down.

Trey didn't help matters. "Braden, shut the hell up. You're embarrassing yourself."

"I didn't say anything!"

"You didn't have to. That hangdog look said it all." As Braden slumped into his seat, Trey shook his head and got up to grab a disc from the TV stand. He popped it into the Xbox. "Let's watch a movie. Braden grabbed a couple of action movies from the rental box earlier."

"As long as it doesn't have The Rock in it," I said.

Kage balked. "You got a problem with Dwayne?"

"No, but Braden has a thing for him. It's a little ridiculous."

"We had to cut him off," Trey concurred, sitting back down on the sofa and hugging a throw pillow to his belly. "No more Dwayne in this house."

Braden smirked. "It's true. But you gotta admit he's fucking awesome. Right?"

"Hell, yeah," Kage agreed. "I met him once in Vegas. Supernice guy."

"Really?" Braden nearly went through the ceiling.

"Yes, really. I'll watch The Rock with you anytime. Just let me know when."

Braden beamed at Kage before shooting me a smug duck-pout, which I fired right back at him.

I'd been expecting to massage Kage's shoulders as he sat between my legs, but he surprised me when he stretched out on the carpet, his massive frame blanketing half of the living room floor. I hesitated for a long moment.

"You coming down here, or what?" he prompted. "This is not exactly the five-star service I expected from you, baby."

His use of the endearment was not lost on me. I just didn't know if he'd said it on purpose.

I dropped to my knees and crawled up beside him, leaning across his body and trying to work both of his shoulders evenly, which was a challenge considering his size. My arms, hands and fingers were contorted into odd, cramp-inducing angles. "I could give you a more even shoulder rub if we got back the way we were, with me in the chair and you in front of me."

"Straddle my waist," he said.

"Pardon me?"

He chuckled and stripped his t-shirt over his head, tossing it to the side.

I groaned. "You don't even know how to keep a fucking shirt on, do you? You'll find any excuse you can to show off your body."

"Shut up and climb on," he said. "And watch the side bruise."

I did as he ordered, not daring to look and see if my friends were watching. Trey had skipped over the previews, and the movie had started, so I hoped their attention was already claimed by the TV. Kage didn't even wince as my leg slid over his bruise, but I muttered an apology anyway.

All too soon, it became clear that the feel of his body between my legs was way too reminiscent of other things, and I found myself fighting the urge to grind against him. My dick was getting hard, and it wouldn't calm down no matter how many times I told it this was not the time or place. I wondered if Kage was thinking the same kinds of thoughts, if my being on top of him was making him hard, and if he'd done this on purpose.

The words I'd said earlier to Braden came back to me. *Nothing he does is ever accidental.*

"Kage…" I began, but I wasn't sure what I was going to say to him. I'd told him on the way to school that he could do whatever he wanted as far as announcing our relationship was concerned, so I couldn't very well complain about that again.

"Yesss?" His voice was lazy and contented. And sexy as hell.

"Never mind." I wrapped my fingers around his bulging deltoids and squeezed, digging my fingers in to work the muscles loose. Kage's answering groan was pure sex to my ears, making me go all needy. My skin, my arms, my groin— every inch of my body ached to be in contact with him. The feeling of helpless attraction served to underscore the difference between us and my roommates. Both Trey and Braden had practically made out with their women several times during the day, right in front of us, yet we had to pretend we didn't even care about each other. The knowledge sank deep into my gut and lodged there, sickening me. For the first time, I really understood what had been eating at Kage. Before, I'd just been concerned about getting his attention, getting laid, and wrapping my head around the fact that it was a man whose attention I was craving. Now that he was officially mine, I needed more. His attention and the few private moments we could grab were no longer enough for me. I wanted it all. The whole boyfriend package.

The suggestion in my movements was subtle but clear. Massage technique turned into touches that were slightly too intimate to be platonic. The change was more cerebral than physical, but he picked up on it, and his hips angled up in response. A quick hello from his body to mine, and that's all it took for me to throw caution to the wind.

I lowered my position until I was sitting squarely on the muscular swell of his ass. Then I started running my hands up and down his back, leaning heavily on my arms on the upstroke, and sitting back fully onto his ass on the downstroke. After a few passes, my movements had morphed into a smooth roll-and-thrust, the ridge of my erection skimming along the crevice between those tempting mounds. I was just four— Kage was commando, so make that three— layers of fabric and a bottle of lube away from going for it.

My mind threw out possible scenarios, all of them dirty and ending in someone getting fucked. In private or in front of my roommates, foreplay or just getting right to business, Kage topping or me topping. The way his ass was looking and feeling right then, I was leaning toward the latter.

Right in the midst of my sexual meltdown, Kage did a quarter twist beneath me, grabbed onto my arm to stabilize me, and rolled over. We ended up in the same position, with me straddling him, only now he was on his back. I shuddered, fighting the urge to attack him with every ounce of pent-up desire that was churning inside me. Before I could do any more second-guessing, Kage snaked his big hand around the back of my head and pulled me down until his lips tickled the shell of my ear. He ran his other hand around to cup my

KAGE UNMASKED | MARIS BLACK

ass, fingers anchoring between my cheeks, and crushed his solid erection so hard against mine it made me gasp.

"Are you trying to tease me in front of your friends?" He asked against my ear, his voice heavily laced with desire. "You're trying to make me lose control, aren't you?"

"I think it's the other way around." I ground down on him even harder, trying to press him through the floor. "But that's okay. I'm good with it."

He released my head enough to get his mouth onto mine, and then we were devouring each other with a breathless hunger, our lips crashing together so savagely I thought we'd draw blood. I attempted to get a pelvic thrust in down below, but Kage had our bodies wedged so tightly together, I groaned with the exertion. That only made Kage more frenzied as he licked into my mouth and punched his hips up into me. We were trying so hard to get at each other, only fusion could have gotten us any closer.

Braden's alarmed wail was a mosquito buzz on the fringe of a malaria haze. A distinct threat, but one I was too far gone to worry about.

"Oh, for heaven's sake," Trey groaned. "I knew that massage was a bad idea. Do I need to go get a bucket of cold water to throw on you two?"

I lifted my head, feeling my bruised lips and my lust-heavy eyelids. "Sorry," was all I could think to say. That thing I liked to call a brain had already flipped around the *Out to Lunch* sign.

Kage laughed, and the sound made everything below my waistband tingle. "Nah, we'll take it to the bedroom. If we keep going out here, we'll have to charge you guys admission."

"Uh…" Braden looked from Trey, to us, and back again. His expression wouldn't have looked out of place in the aftermath of an alien ship landing.

I was strangely calm when I finally found my voice. "Why are you looking at us like that? Haven't you ever seen two guys kiss before?"

Braden's Adam's apple bobbed furiously as he attempted to swallow the news. "No, actually I haven't. Not like that. It didn't look… Well, it looked kinda—"

"Gay," Trey supplied. Bless his heart.

"Are they joking?" Braden choked out. "Is this a joke? They're pranking us, right?"

I wanted to pat Trey on the back for the incredulous look he aimed at Braden. "You and I are best friends. Would you make out with me for a joke?"

"Hell no."

"All right, then. Neither would they. Jesus Christ, too bad all your dad's money can't buy you a fucking clue."

Kage suddenly rolled me beneath him, looking down at me at close range, his pupils blown wide with lust. "I'm gonna go to bed, babe. You need a minute with them?"

I absolutely did not need a minute with them. I wanted to have sex, not deal with my friends. I meant to tell him so, but I nodded instead, mesmerized by the way the light from the TV strobed across his handsome features.

"Wake me up if I'm asleep," he said, planting a sloppy kiss on my lips before hopping up. He was a walking spank bank standing over me, trying and failing to be discreet when he adjusted the straining boner that had pitched a tent in his pants. "And don't be too long. You and I have got unfinished business from earlier today. Remember?"

I did remember.

My stomach was doing backflips as I leaned up onto my elbows and watched him walk away, his fine ass hugged by my tight sweats. When he'd disappeared down the hall and into my bedroom, I turned reluctantly back to my friends.

"What the heck was that all about?" Braden demanded.

I shrugged, fighting a satisfied grin.

"I don't get it." Braden stared down the hall after Kage, as if getting another look at him might clear up the mystery that had his head tied in knots.

"What don't you get?" Trey practically yelled. "Let me spell it out for you. Your idol is gay, and he's sleeping with your roommate. Fucking two plus two, man."

"But—" Braden fixed me with a look that was almost… hurt.

"You're not going all homophobic on me, are you? I'm still the same guy I was five minutes ago."

"I've got to process this." Braden rubbed his face, clearly disturbed.

"You promised you wouldn't tell anyone Kage's business," I reminded Braden.

He scowled at me. "Fuck you, Atwood. Just because I'm a little surprised doesn't mean I'm gonna go running my mouth. I'm not a dick."

"Actually, you kinda are," I said. "But we love you anyway."

"Speak for yourself," Trey said, but we both knew he didn't mean it. Since he'd moved in, Trey and Braden had formed a special bond that didn't include me, probably because I'd never been addicted to video games.

"So you two are... *fucking* each other?" Braden's pained expression pleaded with me to tell him he was wrong. That hell no, Kage and I were absolutely not fucking, and Trey was absurd for even suggesting such a thing.

I shrugged. "Mostly he fucks me. But yeah."

Braden blinked slowly. "What about Vanessa Hale? She was cheating on you with him, right? They were getting engaged, and you were devastated."

Trey groaned. "Braden, please. Two plus two again, dude. It was Kage cheating on him, not Vanessa." Trey glanced at me, alarmed that maybe he'd just said the wrong thing.

"Don't worry about it. I'm over it. He has to do shit for publicity, you know? They're close friends, but he doesn't love her." I was embarrassed at the bitterness I heard lacing my own voice.

"Does he love *you?*" Braden blurted.

I glanced down the hall to make sure Kage wasn't listening before answering quietly, feeling like a teenager at a slumber party. "He hasn't actually said the words, but he acts like he does."

Braden shook his head, and I fancied I could hear marbles rattling around in it. "How long has this been going on? You were just with Layla a few months ago."

"Well," I began, trying to work out the details in my own mind. "I guess it technically started that night we went to the MMA event at Phillips Arena. I met Kage there, and within a couple of weeks I was on my way out to Vegas to be his intern."

"Your mysterious summer job," Trey said.

"I still can't believe it." Braden jumped up and started pacing the floor. "Michael Kage is gay."

"Oh, but you have no problem believing I am?"

He frowned at me. "How long have you been in the closet?"

"What?" I tried to wrap my head around the question. "I've never been in the closet, Braden. I mean I lied about Vanessa, but you gotta understand. Kage is a celebrity. It's not like I could just go around announcing it to everybody." I knew I was sugarcoating in my own favor— that I had technically been misleading people for more reasons than that one, and would probably have continued to do so indefinitely. But it was a moot point now, since Kage had just basically seduced me in front of my friends and left me to take the heat.

In fact, it was some nerve he had to out us and then escape to the relative safety of the bedroom. "Kage!" I yelled, becoming more agitated as things got harder to explain.

It took him all of three seconds to make it back into the living room, pulling his borrowed sweatpants into place as he approached. "What is it?" His muscles were tense, as if he was ready to whip some ass for me.

"Why did you run off and leave me to explain everything? Now Braden's accusing me of being in the closet, and saying you were cheating on me with Vanessa."

"I never cheated on you," he said. "And I'm sorry. I didn't mean to make it seem like I was running off and leaving you alone. I just figured they were your friends, and you'd want to deal with it in your own way, in private."

"Thanks," I snapped. "I appreciate it. Meanwhile, you're in there getting started without me."

"I guess leaving you wasn't the right thing to do." He took a step into my personal space and faced my friends. "Do you guys have a problem with this? I thought you'd be supportive of Jamie. Did I read you wrong?"

Both Trey and Braden shook their heads, and I saw Braden swallow.

"I've got no problem with it," Trey said. "I already knew anyway."

"Really?" Braden regarded him with a stunned expression. "How?"

"Because I'm not blind. Look at Jamie's neck. Did you think he'd suddenly developed a half-dollar-sized strawberry birthmark?" He offered Kage an apologetic smile. "Don't mind Braden. He's dense as hell, but he's basically a good guy. When he gets his tiny brain cells wrapped around this whole thing, he'll be fine with it."

Braden glared at Trey. "You know, insulting my intelligence doesn't actually make you smarter. Or better looking."

Trey glared back.

67

"Listen," Kage interrupted. "Apparently, I didn't handle this well. Let me clear everything up so you two can quit bickering. Jamie and I are together, if that wasn't obvious. I can make it more obvious if you want."

"No, thank you," Braden said quickly.

"Alright then." He stepped behind me and snaked an arm around my waist, pressing his body against my back. "So you guys understand that this is something you're going to be seeing from now on."

They nodded.

"And Jamie thinks it's a bad idea for the media to find out about us, so if either one of you says anything to anyone outside of this house before we give the go-ahead, I'll be forced to hurt you. I don't want to, so please don't make it come to that."

The room was silent. No one moved.

Then I broke the silence by spinning around in his embrace and pressing a kiss to his warm throat. "You're scaring the shit out of my friends."

"I just want them to understand."

"I've got it," Trey said.

"Me, too." Braden shoved his hands into his pockets. "I won't say a word to anyone. And just for the record, I don't have a problem with you guys. I'm just shocked, that's all. Give me some time to get used to it, alright? We're cool."

"Good." Kage tightened his grip on my waist. "Because I'm not going anywhere."

I loved the sound of that so damn much. But at the same time, something nagged at my brain— a little voice that said our happily ever after was just a naïve fantasy, and that all too soon Kage and I would be flushed out into the harsh spotlight of reality.

I didn't know whether our fragile relationship could survive that.

Kage pulled me toward the bedroom. "Time to say goodnight to your friends, college boy."

"Goodnight, friends." I smiled wickedly.

"Hey, I've just got one request," Braden said. "How about not making too much noise?"

Kage laughed. "I'd suggest you turn the TV up, then. Jamie's a screamer."

I punched him hard in the arm, and then he shoved me toward the room, causing me to stumble. We were both laughing, and just as we disappeared into my bedroom, the TV volume shot up. That made us laugh even harder.

"CAN I TOP you again?" Jamie crawled across the floor to kneel up between my legs where I was sitting on the bed, putting his mouth on me through the fabric of the sweatpants and staring up at me with those big brown fuck-me eyes.

I shuddered at the feel of his hot mouth on me, and the tightening of my balls as his finger slid brazenly between my legs to press against my hole. "Sure," I said, swallowing a groan. "But you're going to have to earn it."

"What can I do?" He kept moving his mouth and his fingers, manipulating my cock with his lips, squeezing it and nipping playfully at it until the fabric of the sweats was wet and I was painfully hard. His finger teasing at my hole had me tightening on the memory of him inside of me, and I knew I wanted him there again. Someday. "I'm ready right now," he said. "Look what I've got for you."

He dropped his hand to his own dick, stroking it just for me, inviting me to watch. The shape of it was so perfect moving in and out of his fist, the pink head disappearing into his hand only to reappear on the downstroke. I wanted it in my mouth, but at the moment, the sight of him pleasuring himself was even more tempting.

He was so beautiful, every inch of him perfectly formed. Pouty lips, cut chest and abs, trim hips, muscled thighs. I would have been content to be locked in a room forever just worshiping him. He didn't understand that, though. I could tell in the way his eyes lit up when I complimented him. He had no idea just how perfect he was.

At that moment I was torn between wanting to kiss him, watch him jerk off, fuck him, or let him keep on teasing my back door with his wicked fingers. But those lips... "Get up here and kiss me," I told him.

"Wait. Get rid of those pants." As I moved to slide them off, he grabbed the lube, poured it into his hand. Then slathered it between my bare ass cheeks, slicking up every bit of skin he could reach. I felt it running down onto the sheets.

I laughed. "You're making a mess, Jamie."

"I don't care," he panted. "Don't try to distract me. I'm fucking you tonight."

My eyebrows shot up. "You think so?"

"I know so."

"And how do you plan to earn that privilege? I thought we might have another round of sparring. First one to get a submission gets the other one's ass."

He shook his head and pushed the tip of his finger against my slick hole, just barely breaching it. I sucked in a breath.

"I'm not fighting you, Kage. We both know you'll win."

"So what are you planning to do? I'm not just gonna give it up to you." I was teasing him, and we both knew it. I was already about halfway to giving it up.

"I figured I'd just do it the old fashioned way, by seducing you. Getting you so hot for my dick you won't even be able to refuse."

"You must think very highly of your seduction skills."

"Oh, I do." He bent to my cock and ran the tip of his tongue through the bead of precum waiting there for him, then dropped a soft kiss on the head of my dick and smiled. His lips followed the curve as he sucked the head into his mouth, teasing me mercilessly with his tongue before attempting to swallow it whole. I gasped as his head bobbed up and down over my lap, and my dick swelled and strained within the sweet suction of his mouth.

"Jamie, Jamie…" I groaned as I wound my fingers tightly in his hair and yanked, putting him exactly where I wanted him. The need to guide him was overwhelming, because it meant taking control, and I hadn't learned yet how to give that up. Not when it came to sex.

I held his head stationary and fucked up into his mouth, delighting at the sloppy sounds his lips made every time they lost suction and came off the head of my cock. I loved watching that pretty mouth take my cock, especially when he looked up at me like he was at that moment, his eyes wide open, giving that slutty look as he worked me so deliberately with his lips. He was clearly determined to blow my mind, and God was it ever working. I shuddered in ecstasy.

"For a straight guy, you sure have turned into a dirty little cocksucker, you know that? You have no idea how much you're turning me on right now."

He moaned around my dick, because that's all he could do with his mouth stuffed full.

Just when I thought I couldn't take much more of his torturous mouth, he pulled off with a loud pop that resonated in my belly and my balls. "Slide up onto the bed and spread your legs," he said. I started to protest, but he pounced on me and devoured my mouth with a flurry of hungry kisses that left me lightheaded. The tongue that had just been teasing my dick was now tasting my lips.

I spread my legs for him and he slid up between them. I felt his hot cock rubbing against mine, his balls nudging mine, making me so hard. I was torn, because I wanted to take him so badly— lived to take him— and yet, I could feel the twinge in my ass, and I wanted to beg for him to take me instead. Only him. I'd never wanted anyone else in that way. My thing had always been to dominate and conquer, but when I looked up into his gorgeous face, so full of need, I just wanted to give him everything I had.

He wasn't domineering, and he wasn't an alpha. He was a quiet conqueror. He must have been, because he'd certainly conquered me.

As he rutted against me, I could feel the precum soaking our cocks. Jesus, there was a lot of it this time. It was because this was such a new feeling for both of us, and we were needy bastards. Jamie wasn't shy about trying to top me, like he had been the first time. He was insistent as he began to prod at my quivering hole with the tip of his cock. I could tell he wasn't altogether sure if I'd been serious about making him earn it. I'd made him doubt my desire for him, and it was time to change that.

I spread my legs even farther, opening up for him as much as I could. Then I grabbed onto the back of his head and pulled him down to kiss him. "You're killing me, baby," I mumbled through fevered kisses. "I want to feel that beautiful cock inside me."

He groaned against my lips. "That's all I needed to hear."

He pushed into me, both of us slick from lube and precum, and the feeling that washed over me was like nothing I'd ever felt. He sucked at my throat as he pounded into my ass, drowning me in sensation until I thought I would explode.

"I'm not gonna last long," he gasped. "You feel so good, and *God*, I love fucking you."

"That's okay, baby. You come whenever you're ready."

He started to shudder, and the intense pleasure on his face as he came was enough to almost take me there. But I wasn't ready. I wanted to come inside him, too. So as soon as he had filled me with his seed, I returned the favor. I pulled him on top of me and, using some of the various fluids covering our bodies, I slicked him up and slammed in.

"Baby, you turn me inside out. I'm about to blow you through the ceiling when I come." And that's all it took. Three strokes and some dirty talk, and I was nutting all up in him.

When we were both sated, we didn't bother to shower. It felt nice just to be natural, and now that everyone in the house knew we were a couple, there was no need to worry. I slept like a baby curled up in Jamie's arms.

5

(JAMIE)

Mom WAS THRILLED that Kage and I were coming for dinner. I knew she would cook enough to feed an army, and that my sister and her fiancé would be there. I dreaded that, but it couldn't be helped. If Kage and I were going to have a relationship of any kind, he needed to get used to seeing my family at least every once in a while. Hell, I would have bent over backward to get to know his uncle if the man hadn't made it a point to hate my guts. Not to mention, the surveillance thing was sort of a deal breaker.

As I maneuvered the Rover into the driveway, Mom came running out, letting the storm door catch my dad in the forehead as he tried to follow. "Fuck," I heard him scream. Mom, turned and fired off one of her laser beam looks of condemnation, and he yelled, "Fudge!"

She grabbed me and pulled me into a breath-stealing bear hug. "Oh, you look so good, baby! I missed you so much!" Ever since she'd emerged on the other side of her double mastectomy cancer-free, she'd been euphoric.

"Mom, have you been dipping into Dad's office drawer again?"

The woman slapped my face. Like literally slapped my face. It wasn't a hard slap, but it shocked a yelp out of me. Then, without even acknowledging that she'd assaulted me, she moved on to Kage, standing on tiptoe and throwing her arms around his wide shoulders.

"You gonna slap me, too?" he asked with a grin.

I rubbed absently at my jaw. "Don't do it, Mom. He likes it."

"I'm sure he does," she said, hooking her arm in his.

Kage and I shared a *what-the-fuck* moment over the top of her head. Then my dad was upon us, giving me a noncommittal man hug before trying to crush the bones of Kage's right hand.

"Good to see you again, Mr. Atwood." Kage's obvious attempt at suburban politeness warmed my heart, even though I knew how badly behaved he was beneath the facade. His duplicitous nature was such a turn-on for me, even with my parents buzzing around us.

The outfit he'd chosen at the mall wasn't helping matters. He wore a simple white Henley that somehow covered and accentuated his muscles at the same time, and fitted wool dress pants in a bold heather-gray. The cuffed pants bunched just at the tops of his tobacco-colored ankle boots, giving the impression of effortless sophistication. Like his fighting, his shopping style was efficient and accurate— "I'll take this, and this, and this." Meanwhile, I'd stressed over my own decisions, waffling between khaki or black pants, dress shoes or ankle boots, button-down or sweater. In the end, he'd chosen for me: skinny black leathers, a navy sweater, and boots similar to his. "I love you in blue," he'd whispered while the sales girl rang up our purchases. He'd worn his hair loose, an elastic snapped around his wrist on standby.

We looked damn good, and damn out of place, standing in front of my parents' house.

Dad sized us up and grunted, striking a Superman pose with his hands on his hips. Either he'd lost weight or he was sucking in his gut, because his peach golf shirt didn't seem to be as filled out as usual.

I patted his belly. "Looking good, old man."

He shrugged it off, a twitch at the corner of his mouth the only indication that he was pleased with the compliment. Then he wandered around to the back of the Rover, inspecting it.

"What a beautiful SUV," Mom said. "Kage, is this yours, or did you boys rent one for the weekend? I know Jamie's car isn't exactly luxurious."

"Or safe," Kage said. "That funeral on wheels is gone. This is Jamie's new car."

Mom looked like she'd sucked a lemon. "Don't tell your fa—"

"What did you say?" Dad was suddenly at my side, his eyes narrowing. "This thing belongs to Jamie?"

"Yeah, Dad. Isn't it great?" I smiled, willing him to be nice, and pretend to go along with it even though he was probably in the process of mentally disowning his gay-hooker son.

He pulled open the driver's side door and ran his hand over the steering wheel, then the leather seat. "This thing's got all the bells and whistles, huh?"

"Just about," Kage said. "We didn't get the entertainment package, which was basically a media player and LCD screens. Neither one of us watch movies that much."

"Smart man. It's good you didn't let them sell you something you don't need. Hop into the passenger seat with me and let me take it for a spin around the neighborhood."

Without another word to us, the two of them climbed into *my* SUV and left. Mom and I just looked at each other and went into the house. "I cooked dinner," she said.

"You wouldn't be my Mom if you didn't cook way too much food."

She slipped her hand into an oven mitt and pulled a casserole out of the oven. "It's how I show my love, Jamie."

"I know what it means." I leaned on the counter and peered into each of the dishes she already had grouped there. "I actually cooked for Kage this morning."

She turned and stared at me, a goofy smile on her face. "Does that mean you're in love?"

"Mom." I rolled my eyes and bit into a biscuit-wrapped lil smokies. Even burning the skin off of my tongue couldn't diminish the ecstasy. "Mmm, my favorite."

"Hey, don't eat yet. Everyone's not here."

"But I have to eat at least four of these before Kage gets here. I don't want him to see how weak I am."

"You eat whatever you want today, baby. I didn't go to the trouble of cooking you all this good food just for him to tell you that you can't eat it. Let him try it in front of me. He won't know what hit him."

"I hope you're not really planning on hitting a professional fighter, Mom. That would be embarrassing for everyone involved."

She waved off the notion with a flick of her wrist. "Oh, he wouldn't hit a lady."

I cocked my head and ate an entire biscuit, considering while I chewed, realizing I wasn't altogether sure if Kage would hit a lady or not. I didn't *think* he would, but he was so unpredictable. I could almost imagine him knocking Layla on her ass if she kept fucking with him. But then, if he hadn't done it at breakfast, she was probably safe.

Mom stepped in front of me, running a fingertip delicately along the underside of my jaw. "Somebody ought to hit him for marring my baby's beautiful skin, though."

My face went red enough to match the mark. "Sorry, I forgot about that." I turned abruptly away from her and ran right into my little brother.

"Jamie!" Paul squealed, attempting to engage me in a high five. I failed him, catching the edge of his wrist with my pinky finger. "Is Kage here?"

"He and Dad took my new SUV for a drive. They'll be right back."

"I watched him fight Diaz, you know. Well, I had to wait till today to watch the highlights on YouTube, because Dad wouldn't let me get the pay-per-view." He poked his plump bottom lip out, his freckled face flushed with excitement.

"Are you fucking serious? Dad wouldn't get the pay-per-view?"

"Don't you say that word in this house." Mom shook a serving spoon at me, and a chunk of broccoli casserole flew off of it and landed on my shirt. I grimaced and flicked it off onto the floor, inspecting my new shirt for damage. "Pick that up," she ordered.

I retrieved the goop from the linoleum and begrudgingly walked it over to the trash can. "Paul, next time I'll buy the pay-per-view for you."

"How can you pay for anything?" Mom asked. "Are you working?"

"I can afford it. Don't worry about it." I mentally chastised myself, realizing that I was thinking of Kage's money as my own. What had happened to me?

"I certainly will worry about it. Your father and I are paying your expenses at school, and you're talking about spending your own money on a TV fight for your brother. Did you know those things cost fifty dollars? For one TV show."

"But it's not just any TV show," Paul argued. "It's special. It's Jamie's boyfriend fighting."

Mom and I both turned to stare at Paul. I was busy trying to picture Mom and Dad sitting my little brother down and explaining my situation to Paul, when Mom piped up in a shocked voice. "Where did you hear that?"

Paul took a wary step back, buckling under our intense scrutiny. "That Kage is Jamie's boyfriend? I heard Dad telling Jennifer that she ought to dump that deadbeat Chase. He said, 'It's bad when your brother has a better boyfriend than you.'"

"Yesss!" I did a celebratory fist pump. "Thank you, Paul. You heard that, right Mom?"

"Yes. I heard how your father needs to watch what he's saying when there are little ears around." Mom clicked her tongue and went back to arranging the food.

"These ears aren't too little anymore." I grabbed Paul in a headlock and pulled on one of his ears while he struggled. "This big guy is ten years old already. Can you believe that?"

"Almost eleven," he grunted from within the headlock.

The storm door banged in the living room. I let go of Paul and looked up excitedly, expecting to see my dad and Kage returning, not even trying to hide my disappointment when it turned out to be Jennifer and Chase. "Oh, fu— fudge. Who invited them?"

"What's the matter, Jamie? Are we not big enough celebrities for you?"

"No, actually you're not. I'm jet-setting now."

"Kage is here." Paul stuck out his tongue at Jennifer. "You said I wouldn't get to see him again, but guess what? He and Dad are driving Jamie's new SUV."

"Really, Jamie? A chromed-out black Escalade with tinted windows? Like that doesn't scream drug dealer."

"It's not an Escalade, for your information. It's a Range Rover."

Chase, a pickup truck enthusiast who took ostentatious to a whole new level, looked at me like he was concerned for my soul. "Dude, you spent almost ninety grand, and you don't even know what you got?"

Oh, hell. This was the South. Everyone in the room knew my manhood had just been called into question. I opened my mouth to take up for myself, but my mom beat me to it.

"Jamie's not stupid. It's a Range Rover. It was written plain as day on the front edge of the hood, right above the grille. And I must say, it's very fancy. I'm betting your father drove it all the way to his friend Stuart's house just to show it off." She looked pointedly at me. "Did that thing really cost almost ninety thousand dollars?"

I winced shut my eyes, willing myself not to give in to the need to defend my manhood to Chase. Mom would probably freak when she found out how much Kage had spent on me, and on top of that, Chase was lame. But, of course, pride won out. "Add a one in front of that number." I looked at Chase, hating myself when I said, "Plus tax."

Mom gasped. "You have got to be kidding me. That's more than we paid for this house."

Chase whistled appreciatively. "Guess that wasn't your ride parked at the curb, after all. I ain't never seen an Escalade that cost two hundred grand, and that was definitely an Escalade. I'd stake my life on it."

I rushed to the front door and looked out. The curb was empty. "Was it just sitting there?" I asked. "Like was it parked, running, driving by...?"

"It was idling," Chase said. "It pulled away when we came up, but it was definitely idling in front of this house. Why?"

Jennifer gasped. "Do you think it's the paparazzi?"

I snorted. "I hope the hell not. If it was, we're probably screwed." Then something occurred to me. "Has anyone explained to you guys that no one outside of this house can know about Kage and me?"

"Nobody told me," Paul said. "I was gonna tell my friends at school that I know him, but I haven't said anything. You want me to keep it a secret?"

"Yes, please, buddy."

"Dad already read us the riot act," Jennifer said. "He said I'd be disowned if I said anything."

Chase laughed. "You got off lucky. He said he'd castrate me."

Mom turned away to hide her laughter, but she wasn't fooling anyone.

"I hope that wasn't the paparazzi," Jennifer mused distractedly. "But just in case, I need to go check my hair and makeup." She disappeared to the bathroom while Mom washed a few dishes, and Paul and Chase investigated the food. I wandered to the bay window at the front of the house and peeked out around the edge of the curtain, watching for any sign of a black Escalade. There was a good chance someone was watching my parents' house, and Kage and my dad had been gone long enough for me to get worried.

Paul asked me to play a video game with him, and I sat down and lost myself for a while. Finally, the door opened and in strolled the missing joyriders.

"It's about time." I jumped up from the sofa and met them at the door, my stomach quivering at the sight of Kage running a hand through his hair to get it out of his face, revealing a heart-stopping smile. Here I was freaking out, and he looked so relaxed... with my dad. Hell, even Dad was smiling.

"That's a hell of a ride you have there, son." He clapped me on the shoulder, and I wondered briefly, irrationally, if he meant the car or Kage. "Be sure to keep the oil changed and the tires rotated. Regular maintenance is crucial."

"Do I need to have the oil changed already? You were gone a *long* time." I knew I was showing my apprehension. Now that I was sure the mysterious Escalade hadn't somehow gotten them, I was worried about what they'd talked about. Had they discussed me? Had they argued? Had Dad said anything embarrassing?

"Don't worry about it, babe." Kage kissed me. Right in front of my family, like it was nothing. It wasn't a long kiss, but it was intimate. He closed his eyes and breathed me in as his lips met mine and his hand pressed possessively against the small of my back. And then he was gone, and I was reeling.

I did a one-eighty spin on my heel, checking to see who'd witnessed the kiss. Everyone, apparently. Five sets of eyes stretched wide, blinked, then looked away... and that was it.

"Food's getting cold," Mom announced. "Ice is in the glasses, though it's melted a bit. Strain it out into the sink if you don't want watered-down tea."

We all swarmed the food. Even Kage sampled everything and went back for seconds of his favorites. I smiled to myself when he grabbed the last three lil smokies from the platter.

Jennifer and Chase were surprisingly well behaved. Chase didn't retire to the TV while the rest of us did the family thing. He hung right with us for a change, and I had to wonder if my dad had given him a talking-to. Or maybe Jennifer wanted to make sure he wasn't found lacking when compared to my boyfriend. I still couldn't believe Dad had said that to her.

Paul asked Kage if he could show him how to do the flying armbar he'd executed so flawlessly on Cristiano Diaz for the win.

"Sure, but Jamie could show you how, too. He submitted me with it the same night I submitted Diaz."

"Really?" Paul's leveled astonished eyes on me.

I blushed. "He's exaggerating. He taught me how to do it, but he's much better at it than I am. I could show you how to do a couple of Judo throws, though."

It was Kage's turn to look astonished. "We haven't worked much on throws. How are you such an expert?"

"Been taking some classes." I shrugged. "No big deal."

Kage continued to stare at me with a little smile on his face. I'd been reluctant to tell him I was training, but he certainly seemed pleased about it. Probably because the cocky bastard knew I'd done it to impress him. Which was sort of true.

After dinner, we all crowded around the sink trying to help. Mom indulged us, even though I could tell we were getting in her way.

As soon as an opening presented itself, I grabbed Kage by the arm and pulled him out into the backyard toward the infamous gazebo of pain. Unfortunately, Jennifer and Chase had already beaten us to it and were making out.

"Dammit," I hissed, stopping abruptly, causing Kage to run into my back.

"What's the matter?" he asked.

"I'm horny, and they got the gazebo."

Kage laughed. "Is this an Atwood family tradition? Dinner followed by dry humping in the backyard?"

"No. It's just..." I turned and cut my eyes up at him, vibrating with sexual need. "You just look so good today. God, your ass looks amazing in those pants, and your muscles in that shirt... *gah*. I just wanna touch you." I thought for a second, then dragged him along again. "Let's go to my room."

"Oh, no." Kage pulled against me. "Hell no. Your dad said we were not to go to your room."

"What?" I pulled again. "Fuck that. We're going to my room, and he'll just have to get over it. We'll be sneaky." Kage reluctantly let me lead him toward my room, but even my attempted stealth didn't stop my dad from catching us.

"Where are you boys headed?" he yelled from the sofa, where he was leaned back beside Mom, supposedly reading a book.

"My room." I laughed. "Kage wanted to see my high school yearbooks."

Kage shot me an evil glare. "Do you *want* him to shoot me?"

Without even looking up from his book, Dad said, "Have you already forgotten what we talked about on the ride?"

"No, sir." Kage smiled wickedly at me. "It was Jamie's idea. I told him it was wrong for us to go to his room, but he said if I loved him I'd do it."

"James…" Dad used *that tone*. The one that said resistance was futile.

"Great," I hissed. "Way to go. Now he hates us both."

"He doesn't hate me. He loves me." Kage crossed his arms, and my eyes dropped to his biceps, so mouthwatering in the thin white shirt.

I licked my lips and forced my eyes to his face. "What the hell did you guys talk about on that drive? This feels suspiciously Stepford, you know?"

"We just came to an understanding. It was nice."

And that was about all I could take of the mystery. Kage and I needed to discuss the status-quo-obliterating ride he and my dad had taken before dinner, so I grabbed his arm again and pulled him to the only safe place I could think of. Through the kitchen, and the laundry room, and into the ten-by-ten pantry Dad had built for Mom when I was in middle school. It was mostly lined with shelves, but there was still plenty of standing room. As long as we kept our voices down, I was confident no one would think to look for us in there.

"What are we doing in here?" Kage scanned the shelves stocked with canned goods, baking items, and cleaning supplies. I closed the door behind me, plunging us into complete darkness, and felt around for the string that dangled from the light fixture in the center of the ceiling. I gave it a tug, and the bulb cast a harsh blue glow over everything. "Are you trying to give me nightmares? This place is nutrition hell. Look at all these starches." He picked up several items, squinting at the labels in the blue gloom. Then he put his hand on a clear container. "Hey, are these Christmas decorations? There's all kinds of stuff in here." He picked up a foam snowman from beside the container and inspected it before putting it back down.

"Will you help me do a Christmas tree this year?"

"Yeah, sure," I said. "Why don't you quit inspecting everything and come over here?"

But Kage had spotted the dry-erase board in the corner. He grabbed the marker from the tray, and in bold blue letters wrote, "Kage wuz here."

I laughed. "How old are you, thirteen? Forget about that stuff and tell me what you and my dad talked about in the car. Because, I've gotta tell you, I'm shocked at how well you two are getting along. You're like the country club son he never had."

He replaced the marker in its tray and stalked over to me. "Well, I don't wanna talk about that." His voice was playful, taunting me as he skated a fingertip lightly over my button fly. "I'd rather talk about what's got you so *wound up*. You like this side of me, yeah?"

"Yes," I breathed. "But only because I know what's underneath. You're like Eddie Haskell on steroids." I pretended to smooth the fabric of his shirt, running my palms over the muscled perfection of his chest, his ribs, his abs. "Of course, you're a lot fucking hotter. This shirt—"

"I wanted you to see." He grabbed on to my hand and clutched it to his chest, his expression earnest. "I can do this for you, Jamie. I can be the family guy."

"But it's not really you."

"Sure it is."

"No." I slid my free hand down the front of his pants and squeezed his dick hard enough to make him gasp. "No, it's not."

"Okay, you win." He spun me around and pushed me into a stand of various mops and brooms, their long wooden handles all clattering loudly against my back.

We giggled silently, doing little more than moving air in the enclosed space, trying to keep from giving ourselves away. Kage gathered the mops and brooms in both fists and moved them to another area before pushing me against the now-empty strip of wall.

I was dizzy, from the limited amount of air circulating in the pantry and from Kage's proximity. Every time he looked at me or touched me, it got a little harder to breathe. The air was already feeling thick and heavy.

"Jesus, it's a thousand degrees in here," I panted, working the tail of his shirt up with my fingers and connecting with the hot flesh of his abdomen, tracing the ridges of his six-pack.

"We survived the sauna," Kage reminded me. "This is nothing."

He ducked down to catch my mouth with his, randomly nipping and licking at me over and over, heedless of art or precision. We were both stupid with want, grabbing and pulling at each other, frantically seeking satisfaction. I opened the front of his pants and worked his cock out with trembling fingers, needing to feel it in my hand, all warm and stiff and powerful. Kage pushed his pants all the way down to his knees to give me better access, then he got me half naked, removing my shirt before expertly freeing each button of my fly and shoving my pants to my knees. When he took my throbbing cock into his hand, a tiny sound escaped my throat.

"Quiet," he whispered. Then we were kissing again as he proceeded to torture me with rough strokes that blurred the line between pleasure and pain, working me over with his unique brand of sexual expertise. I thrust my hips wantonly, fucking up into his tight fist, already chasing my orgasm. It was uncanny the way he knew exactly how to get me to that needy place, where the rest of the world fell away and all that existed was the desperate hunger to feel— pleasure, pain, life, death. In that place, they were all the same.

He shuddered against me, needing me as much as I needed him, but it was almost impossible to concentrate on jerking him off when I kept losing myself to the sensations. Wrapping my arm around his neck and pulling myself closer, I disengaged my mouth from our mad, artless tangle of a kiss and groaned in his ear.

"I want you to fuck me."

"Can't," he panted. "They'll hear."

"I don't care." I stood up on my toes and angled his cock down, positioning the head just below my balls and pulling his hips so that his thick shaft slid right between my thighs.

"You are so fucking slutty today." He rocked his hips, moving his cock incrementally back and forth between my thighs, the ridge of the head teasing my taint in the most wonderful way. He licked my throat, nipped at my jaw, and kissed a hot trail all the way to my mouth, where he sucked my swollen bottom lip. I let out the cry I'd been trying so hard to hold in, and his strong fingers wound around my throat, exerting just enough pressure to demand my attention. My eyes stretched wide, and my body went completely still. "Don't.

Make. A sound," he growled. His uncivilized tone set off a series of quakes in my belly, and I squeezed my thighs to encourage him. "If you even breathe hard, this is over. Do you understand?"

I nodded emphatically, and Kage released me. Then he grabbed a bottle from the back shelf, flipped the top, and squirted a puddle of clear liquid into his hand.

"What is that?" I whispered.

"Liquid coconut oil," he whispered back. At my horrified expression, he added, "It's good for you. Turn around."

"That's my mom's. She cooks with that."

"We're way past the point of worrying about good manners, Jamie." He shoved me down onto the bare concrete floor on my hands and knees, facing the pantry door. Then he lowered himself over me, covering my back with his big frame, his arms running alongside mine. He aligned his cock with my ass and teased me with it before lowering his head to nuzzle against my ear and suck my earlobe into his hot mouth. He was trying to force me to make a noise, but I wasn't about to give him the opportunity to withhold from me again.

I shivered at the low rumble of his voice next to my ear when he asked, "Is this what you want? You want a guy who's twisted enough to get nasty with you on the floor of your mom's pantry? To use your ass with your family so close they might hear?"

He slammed his cock into my ass without warning, burying himself all the way to the root in one brutal stroke that rocked my entire body.

"Ohhh, fuuuck!" My arms buckled from the impact, and I went down onto my elbows on the hard floor. I cried out again, senseless from the shock and from the overwhelming burn of his cock forcing me open.

Kage slapped a hand over my mouth hard enough to hurt. My lips tingled and ached as his strong fingers squeezed me with enough pressure to leave bruises on my skin. I didn't care. I was an animal now— the animal he'd made me— and my desperate pleas for him to fuck me harder were reduced to muffled whimpers within the tight seal of his hand over my face.

I braced myself on bruised elbows as he punched into me with that controlled ferocity that defined him. I was grateful that his hand was there to save me, because I would have given us away. I couldn't shut up, couldn't stop making those pleading sounds, and didn't want to stop.

His cock was so thick and hard inside me, and his movements so increasingly erratic, I knew he was about to blow. And I knew the feel of him emptying inside me would be enough to set me off with one touch. I strained and squeezed, tightening around him and doing my best to make him come.

"God, I love wrecking you," he growled against my ear. Then he leaned up, bringing me with him, until we were both upright on our knees and my back was cinched tightly to his front. His fingers bit into my cheek as he tensed his whole body and came, shooting slick warmth into my body.

The second I felt it, I grabbed onto my aching dick, jerking it furiously, grunting out my own tense climax. Even long after come had splattered up my belly and my chest, I was still fucking my hand, still grinding my ass on Kage with my eyes squeezed shut and his hand covering my mouth. He let me wind down before pulling his slackening cock out of me and releasing my mouth.

"Damn," I said when I could finally speak. "That was pretty intense."

"Too intense for the location," he muttered, helping me up off the floor. "You're becoming an adrenaline junkie like me, baby. You know that, right?"

"Is that okay?" I pulled my wrinkled shirt back on, and we fussed over jizz spots and smears of coconut oil that had found their way onto our clothing.

"I don't know," he said. "If both of us keep pushing the limits and taking chances, who's gonna reel us in?"

"We'll be fine." I gave his biceps an appreciative squeeze. "You're strong enough to keep us both in line."

"If you say so." He wrinkled his nose and smiled. "It smells like sex in here."

"Not for long. My mom keeps the Christmas air freshener in here." I grabbed the can off the shelf and sprayed it around. "There. Now it smells like mistletoe." I gave him a peck on the lips, and we dared to emerge from the pantry and into the real world.

We rounded the corner that separated the kitchen from the living room, and I was suddenly cognizant of exactly what we looked like: two guys who had just fucked in the pantry. Sweaty hair, flushed skin, Kage had obvious pit stains, my shirt was rumpled to hell and back. We were both still breathing a little faster than normal.

Kage glanced at me, then did an obvious double take, his eyes going wide. A little smile tipped the corner of his mouth.

"What?" I whispered.

He swiped at his mouth, as if he was trying to tell me I had something on mine. I reached up and ran my fingers around my lips, but he just shook his head. Looking guilty as hell, he clasped his hands behind his back in an uncharacteristically formal manner and turned his gaze back toward the living room, where most of my family was gathered. Everyone was staring at us in a way that made me even more uncomfortable than I already was.

"Where did you two get off to?" Mom asked, getting up from the couch and coming to stand in front of us. Dad got up and followed, and I nearly buckled under their scrutiny.

Ignoring her question, I put on the biggest smile I could muster. "So I guess we'll be going now." It's not even close to what I'd meant to say, but standing there facing them all, I found that I just wanted to get away.

Mom frowned. "I thought you two were going to stay the night. Jamie, your room is just like you left it, and we made up the guest room for Kage." She stepped closer to me, cocking her head to the side and squinting her eyes right at my mouth.

Fuck. I definitely had something on my face. I ran my fingers around it once more, wishing I had checked myself in a mirror before coming out to face people.

"Actually, we're going to have to decline the invitation," Kage announced loudly, shifting my mother's attention from me to him. "I only have one more night in town before I have to leave for two weeks, and we're not going to waste it in separate rooms. Gotta get every bit of loving in that we can, you know?"

Mom swooned, and Dad literally reached over and covered her ears. Even without a mirror, I knew my face had just gone fire engine red.

"I'm sorry, honey." Dad told mom before shooting Kage an accusing glare. "That was just uncalled for."

Kage was adorably bewildered by our reactions, and though I was horrified, I had the strangest urge to throw my arms around him. He turned to my dad. "I don't understand. I thought we were being honest. At least that's what you said on our drive just a little while ago. That we were going to be straight with each other from here on out, no secrets."

"There's a fine line between honesty and TMI, son. Trust me, that was TMI."

Kage balked. "I didn't realize the subject of sex was taboo. You're the one who brought it up to me, Mr. Atwood. You told me that Mrs. Atwood doesn't believe in premarital sex, so the two of you don't allow your children to sleep with their boyfriends and girlfriends under your roof. Which is fine. You're just being honest about the way you feel. Now I'm being honest about how I feel. I think it's pretty obvious in this day and age that two adults who are officially dating are also having sex. If I have the choice, I'm always going to choose to sleep with Jamie. According to your rules, that means either getting married or staying somewhere else for the night. And since this isn't Vegas, where we can just run down to the corner chapel, I guess we're leaving. I'm not trying to be rude or mean, and I'm sorry Mrs. Atwood if I embarrassed you."

I have to say, I was proud of Kage. He'd honored my dad's request to be honest and to not keep secrets. The fact that Dad hadn't been prepared for the reality of that request wasn't Kage's fault. Not to mention he was such a *man*, and that was so sexy. I stepped close to his side, a silent show of support.

"It's okay, Michael." Mom smiled, having officially recovered from her shock. "I really wish you boys would change your minds and stay here, but I understand. I don't get to see my son often enough."

Kage squeezed my shoulders. "I feel exactly the same, Mrs. Atwood."

Dad's face had softened, and he moved to lean against the kitchen counter. "Well, don't forget the other things we talked about."

Kage gave an answering wink, and suddenly I was dying to get to the Rover and find out what that was all about. I'd meant to get the story in the pantry, but things went a little haywire.

After we were on the road again, I asked Kage for the details.

"We talked about serious things: the future, my intentions toward you, marriage. Real family-type shit. It was nice."

"Yeah?" Warmth bloomed in my chest. "You said good things?"

"Very good things." He gave me a side glance, looking so damn sexy driving our new SUV and smiling at me like he knew a juicy secret. "Of course there's no telling how he feels about me now."

"Why? Because of what you just said in there?"

"No, because of this." He flipped my visor down in front of my face, aiming the mirror right at me, and what I saw in my reflection made me gasp out loud.

There in bright blue marker were Kage's fingerprints, along with a splotchy partial rendering of his fingers. Apparently the marks hadn't been visible in the dim blue light of the pantry, so Kage hadn't noticed them until we were already in the living room.

"Dammit." I glared at him. "You just had to mess with that fucking marker, didn't you?" I scrubbed at my mouth, but none of the ink came off. "God, do you know how embarrassing this is? I just stood there looking like a moron with your hand print on my face, Kage."

He shrugged, holding up a marker-stained hand and looking contrite. "Well, at least it's your color. Have I mentioned how much I like you in blue?"

6

AFTER KAGE LEFT for Vegas, I was lost again. He was going to be attending a training camp to help get Jason Kinney prepped for a fight coming up in two weeks, and I was stuck trying to pay attention in class. The school thing was getting old when all I wanted to do was spend time with my boyfriend.

Those things that he'd said about talking to my father and about marriage had really hung around in the forefront of my mind. I was giddy with thoughts of what a future with Kage might be like. And honestly, at that point I couldn't have imagined a future without him. It was as if he'd walked right in and taken over, embedding himself in the most crucial spot, becoming the heart of my existence. I loved him so much that it didn't even occur to me anymore that he might not feel the same way.

He'd never actually said those three little words that everyone wants to hear, but he'd done so much more, and said things that touched me in ways not even those words could. I cherished everything about him, even his flaws. And that was really saying something, because the guy was forty kinds of fucked up. There was so much about him that was still a mystery, it blew my mind to think that I'd given myself over to him. Kage was like a roller coaster ride—thrilling, but scary as hell. So how was it that he could make me feel so damn secure?

I knew the rest of the world didn't see him the way I did. Very few people could get past the rough exterior, because he didn't let them. It made me feel special that I got to see the vulnerable boy behind the mask. The one who wanted to impress my father, and who cried in his sleep from nightmares about his brother. I hurt so much for him, and yet I couldn't help him if I didn't know what the problem was.

In his last nightmare, he'd woken up saying he'd just killed his brother. I knew that couldn't be true, that it had to be some distortion in his dream, because that's what dreams did. They took real things and distorted them like in a fun-house mirror. Obviously I had never jumped off the top level of a cruise ship, and I hadn't died from my feet touching the ocean floor, but for some reason my dream just kept serving up that same old story. If it had any basis in reality, I couldn't imagine what it might be. So I knew it had to be the same with Kage and the death of his brother. Maybe he just couldn't deal with the loss in his conscious mind, so he kept seeing it through the fun-house mirror of his dreams.

He was going to have to let me in one of these days, though. We couldn't have a lasting relationship if I didn't know the most fundamental events that had shaped his life. There was really nothing significant to know about me. I was boring. Yet I'm sure at some point we'd get around to talking about my summer-camp days, my childhood insecurities, and who I took to my senior prom. But Kage had skeletons in his closet. Hell, he might even have a whole graveyard in there. If he couldn't eventually open up to me about those things, it was going to cause major problems.

At that moment, he was busy with Jason, and I had to admit I was jealous. They were training hard, and Kage had a tendency to get caught up in training and forget to call. I'd gotten used to his disappearances and sketchy communication style, since he'd been that way from the start. He was just as obsessed with me as he was with fighting, and I knew that.

"It doesn't worry you when he doesn't call for a whole day?" Braden asked one night when we were watching TV together.

I shrugged. "Not really. Sometimes I don't contact him, either. We don't have to be up each other's ass all the time."

"That's weird," he said. "If I don't call or text Miranda for a few hours, she's wondering if I'm cheating on her. But I guess I'm the same way. You guys don't get jealous?"

"Actually, we do." I laughed, thinking of some of our more ridiculous jealous moments. "But breaks in communication hasn't been much of an issue. When I first started working for him, he'd disappear for days. No contact whatsoever. Then when he'd show back up, I was just glad to see him."

"Sounds like he got you trained from the beginning."

I laughed. "Maybe. He was gone a lot when we were in Vegas after he got his UFC contract. Most of it was promotion. Some of it was shit his PR people made him do, like being seen on dates with Vanessa Hale."

"Damn." Braden shook his head. "That had to be a mind fuck."

"Yeah, it was. You remember how I got when I saw that picture on the magazine in the grocery store. I was seriously messed up about that. But we've worked things out since then. There's a lot of stuff you don't know, and I'm not at liberty to tell you. Just understand that Kage's life is complicated, and now my life is complicated because of him. The rules don't really apply anymore."

"But what a trade-off. That's a hell of a ride you've got out there in the driveway. No telling what else he'll end up getting you."

"Not to mention the sex. It's like nothing I've ever experienced before. I'm hot for him all the time. He's turned me into a total horn dog."

"I don't need to hear shit like that, Jamie," Braden teased.

I bit my lip, considering how honest I should be with him. Not because I thought he'd run his mouth, but because some of the things I wanted to say made me feel like a lovestruck fool. But then this was Braden, the guy who had just admitted he couldn't go without talking to his girlfriend for a few hours. I decided to confide in him, because I needed to talk to someone. Joy was eating me alive from the inside out.

"Don't laugh, but I think Kage wants to marry me. He and my dad had *the talk* when we went to visit them."

"Really?" Braden looked like he wasn't sure whether to celebrate or not. "That's… well, that's just weird to me, bro. No offense, but it's hard for me to relate. I haven't even talked to Miranda about marriage, and we've been together for longer than you guys have. Do you want to get married?"

"Yes." I'd planned on being nonchalant about it, but there was no way. I grabbed a throw pillow and covered my face to hide the blush and the stupid grin that wouldn't stop. "I'm so in love it's sick."

"Oh, God," Braden groaned. "You sound like a princess who's found her prince."

That knocked the grin right off of my face. I dropped the pillow and scowled at my roommate. "I'm not a girl, Braden. I'm a prince. A prince who has found his king."

Braden narrowed his eyes in thought. "But wouldn't that make him your daddy?"

His words brought yet another blush to my cheeks as I remembered the exchange in the kitchen when Kage stripped off his shirt and asked if he could be my daddy. I didn't even bother answering Braden's question. I told him goodnight and went straight to my room. Then without even turning the light on, I fell into bed and jerked off to thoughts of Kage fucking me on a bejeweled throne. And everywhere else I could think of.

The next day, I was mortified when the property manager approached me just as I got home from class.

"Mr. Atwood, can I have a minute?"

"Yes, sir."

He looked uncomfortable, which made me nervous. "There's just no delicate way to put this. A man paid a visit to me this morning and asked me to suggest to you that you keep your bedroom blinds closed. He said he could see every move you made."

"Oh." Heat rose to my cheeks. "Yes, sir, I'll definitely do that. Do you remember what he looked like?"

"Not really," he admitted. "Just some guy in a suit."

I went inside and closed the door behind me. Then I hurried to my room and shut the blinds. I was embarrassed as hell, but worse than that, I was afraid. I knew it wasn't just anybody who had visited my property manager with such a strange request. It had to be the same person who had sent me the video. I was convinced more than ever that someone was trying to warn me that I was being watched.

I GET TO come out to Vegas again?" I asked Kage over the phone, not even trying to keep the excitement out of my voice.

"Yeah, I'm not going to Jason's fight. The UFC is having this press conference thing here in Vegas, and a bunch of us fighters are gonna be answering questions. They said to be prepared for lots of smack talk, and to not hold back. They're trying to really hype this shit hard— get some of that pro-wrestling drama into it while still keeping it real."

"Do you know who you're going to be fighting next?"

"Not exactly, but I've been talking to some people in the organization, and they basically let me know that they're grooming me, if you know what I mean. They know I'm a badass and can put any of these fighters down, so they're planning to capitalize on that— on the Machine thing."

"They must really like you."

"It's all about selling fights, getting new viewers, stuff like that. They think I'm good main-card material."

I gasped. "You think they'll give you a title shot?"

"Probably not this soon. But I have a feeling it won't be long, and that's gonna piss off a lot of people."

"Really? That would piss people off?"

"You'd better believe it." The sound of voices got louder in the background, presumably the guys in Jason Kinney's fight camp. Kage dropped his voice a notch. "Hey, Jamie?"

"Yes?"

"I can't wait to see you again. Being alone is... well, it sucks. It's getting harder for me."

Silence stretched between us, but I couldn't think of anything to say. It wasn't that I didn't feel the same; I did. It was just that he'd thrown me for a loop. The rare glimpses of his vulnerability always shocked me, because he seemed so confident and strong. It was easy to forget he was just a man— with feelings, and a heart, and weaknesses. The fact that I was a source of weakness for him was especially humbling.

When he figured out I wasn't going to respond, he asked, "How are things going for you?"

"Maybe I can quit school," I blurted. "I mean, if you need some company or something."

"Hell, no. I'm a big boy, Jamie. You're not about to give up your dreams to babysit me. I just miss you, that's all."

"I miss you, too. Believe me. If I wasn't sitting in class waiting for Dr. Washburn to show up, I'd tell you just how much."

He laughed. "Tell me anyway."

"Yeah, right."

"Tell me. Anyway." The rough, commanding quality was so damn sexy, I had no choice but to obey.

"I think about you constantly. I can't even pay attention in class because I'm so horny for you. I fantasize *a lot*."

"What do you fantasize about?"

"Um…" I glanced around to make sure no one was listening, thankful it was an upper level class with enough empty seats that no one was right next to me. Then I gave a hesitant answer. "You."

"Be specific, Jamie. I want to hear some nasty stuff coming out of your mouth. Stuff I can use tonight when I'm lying in bed wishing you were here. Tell me exactly what you want me to do to you when I see you this weekend. Do you want me to make love to you slow and easy?"

"No. I want you to *ruin* me. Make me unfit for anyone else."

"How sweet." His quiet laugh was barely audible. "You don't want me to get all romantic? Light some candles and recite poetry about how much you mean to me?"

I looked around again before replying, "I want you to call me your little slut."

"Is that what you are? My little slut?"

"Yes."

"What do you think I should do with a dirty little slut like you? Push you down? Make you beg for my big cock?"

"Yes. Anything. I'll do anything to get you off." I sank down in the desk and dropped my voice even lower, slipping completely into the fantasy. "Do you want to hurt me, Kage?"

There was a loud noise at the front of the room, the sound of a heavy book being dropped flat onto a desk, and I shot upright in my seat.

"He's here. Gotta go," I whispered before fumbling my phone onto the floor. It flew apart into three pieces— front, back, and battery— effectively ending my call. My heart was racing, my breath coming twice as fast as it should have been.

The girl nearest to me retrieved the pieces of my phone and put them on my desk. "Thanks," I whispered.

The source of the noise had been Dr. Washburn, horsing around to get my attention. Ever since I'd made him late that one time, he'd made sort of a habit of being late at least once a week. It was like I'd loosened up some knot in him, and now he didn't seem quite so uptight. The new, more easygoing Dr. Washburn seemed a lot happier. And I couldn't be positive, but I was pretty sure he'd found a boyfriend. I'd seen him around with a student teacher who was even more of a hipster than Dr. Washburn, and the way they looked at each other was definitely not what you'd call professional.

"Mr. Atwood, are we interrupting an important call?" Dr. Washburn smiled as he pulled his class materials out of his briefcase. "Do you need to reassemble your phone and step out into the hall to talk? We could put the class on hold for you."

Once I'd gotten my breathing under control, I laughed and relaxed back into my desk. "It's okay, Doc. No problem. The guy I was talking to… I'll be spending the weekend with him in Vegas. *Again.*"

"Ahhh… Vegas." Dr. Washburn raised his eyebrows, clearly realizing for the first time that my former boss and I were an item.

In fact, I'd basically just announced to the whole class that I was dating a guy, on purpose and for no other reason than because it felt good, and because I was proud. I wished I could announce exactly who my boyfriend was— pass around a picture of that fine motherfucker and let everyone in class eat their hearts out. How amazing would it feel to have him walk into class right now and lay one on me right in front of everyone?

Something significant had happened since Kage had shown up and spent time with me around my family and friends. There had been a major shift inside me. It hadn't been a smooth shift, but once it happened, everything just clicked into place. I wasn't afraid to let the people in my life know about us anymore. The career thing was still a very real concern, but Kage would have to be the one to make the decisions about that. I wasn't his publicist anymore; I was his boyfriend. I would stand by whatever decision he made, and I wouldn't try to pressure him in either direction.

But now that I was open to other people knowing I was sleeping with a guy, I'd started to feel really guilty about the way I'd treated Kage. With my own fears tainting my perception, I hadn't been able to imagine what freedom would feel like to him. Specifically, the freedom to show off the person he cared about most. He'd told me he was proud of me, but in my limited view, I'd thought he meant he was hot for me. That he had a mad crush on me like I did on him. Now I realized it was more than that.

I couldn't imagine him feeling as proud of me as I was of him, because in my eyes he was the catch, and I was the lucky one. But if he felt even a fraction of the pride I felt, he would want everyone to know about it. Maybe it was shallow, but I sort of felt like he was my trophy boyfriend, and being with him made me a stud. The fact that I was so head over heels in love with the guy made it just that much sweeter.

Sure, I'd felt pride with my girlfriends before. Getting hot girls had never been a problem for me, and making other guys jealous fed my ego like crazy. But this thing with Kage? This was a whole 'nother level. I was playing in the big leagues now, and I was pretty sure I deserved Rookie of the Year.

7

(JAMIE)

WHEN I GOT off the plane, Kage was waiting for me in the limo. He had bought new suits for both of us, so by the time we arrived at the hotel where the press conference was to take place, we were a slick looking duo— the fighter and his assistant. At least those were the official parts we were playing. I almost brought my camera to help make me look more believable in my role of *not-boyfriend*, but in the end I decided it would be a hassle to keep up with a prop. I left it in my luggage, which was delivered to the Alcazar.

The press conference was everything Kage had promised it would be. A multi-tiered platform held three rows of tables, and fighters were seated strategically, several to a table and with plenty of room between them. It hadn't occurred to me before, but a room full of fighters was probably a volatile thing. Emotions were running high, adrenaline was pumping, and there were rivalries to consider—some old, some new. I'd heard it was tough planning a seating chart for a wedding dinner, but I was betting this was even more challenging.

For instance, Cristiano Diaz and Kage were both in attendance. But since Kage had just whipped his ass in front of the whole world, Diaz had a chip on his shoulder. It was clear from the moment his eyes landed on Kage there was going to be trouble. The guy couldn't stop glaring at him. Meanwhile, Kage had no interest in looking at Diaz. I figured it was because he'd beaten him already, so there was no need to worry about him anymore. I did notice Kage watching some of the other fighters, though. The ones who held his attention were the higher-ranking Welterweights he would possibly have to defeat to move forward in the fight for the title. Kage wanted that belt. He didn't talk about it much, but he didn't have to. The man was driven to be the best at every single thing he attempted, so there was no way he wasn't salivating over that belt.

What I found a little surprising was that Kage seemed to be the lowest-ranked fighter by far. Having only fought three UFC fights, he was still a baby compared to the other guys in the room, but he was a star in the making. Anyone could see that. Even the way he carried himself around these men was a testament to his professionalism and potential.

As I watched him climb the steps to the platform and take the seat he was assigned, I couldn't help smiling with pride. That was my man up there.

"Excuse me, mind if I sit here?" A young woman with long blond hair, bright blue eyeshadow, and a nose ring sat down beside me without waiting for my answer. "Are you Michael Kage's assistant? That's what one of the organizers told me."

"That's me. Jamie Atwood, *Assistant*."

I wasn't really in the mood for small talk. I wanted to watch everything. One of the reasons Kage had gotten me into this event was so that I could get some experience. This was just the type of thing I might be doing in the future after I graduated from college. Even more than that, I wanted to keep an eye on Kage. In this atmosphere, it wasn't totally outlandish to imagine that he might get into an altercation. If that happened, I would not hesitate to jump in and start fighting. I wasn't a professional like these guys, but I had a little bit of training, and I had a lot of heart where Kage was concerned. I figured I could at least slow someone down long enough for Kage to beat the shit out of them.

"I'm Farrah. David Grand's girlfriend."

Was it petty of me to feel jealous of her just because she could say that aloud? It was so unfair that I had to pretend, and yet she could just blurt that shit right out.

"Nice to meet you, Farrah." I smiled at her, because it wasn't her fault the situation was messed up. No reason to be unfriendly. "I've never seen your boyfriend fight, but he must be pretty good to be here today."

"He's the number two contender for the Welterweight title. No offense, but I thought you'd know that, being Kage's assistant."

"It's okay. I never said I was a good assistant."

She laughed, and the sound instantly put me at ease. In another life, I might have been attracted to her.

I sought out her boyfriend on the stage just to see what he looked like, and I was underwhelmed. He was average in the face, with a wide jaw and smallish eyes. His nose had been broken, and probably more than once. His body was wide, and I guessed he was probably a good bit shorter than Kage.

When David looked our way, Farrah waved excitedly, and he lifted a hand in response. "Look at him trying to be all cool," she said under her breath. "He's so funny when he gets around these guys."

"Kage and I haven't been to many of these kinds of things, so I'm not sure how he's going to react. If he'll be all aloof or not. If I had to guess, he will be, though. Most people find him to be pretty intimidating, even when we're just hanging out or going shopping."

I realized too late that I was babbling. The urge was strong to brag about my boyfriend, and to let it be known that we were close enough to have funny stories together, too.

Farrah laughed. "Yeah, they can be intimidating. But they can also be big babies."

"I know, right?" My answer was reflex, and I instantly felt bad for insinuating that Kage could be a big baby. I'd never thought of him that way, even when he was clinging to me after a nightmare.

Farrah was in a sharing mood. Unfortunately for her boyfriend, it was his business she wanted to share. "I've never told anybody this, but one time David and I were in a hotel for fight week, and we'd both been drinking. We had a little private time, if you know what I mean, and then I got in the shower to get ready for bed. David got out of bed and finished off the leftovers of our room service meal, but when he went to put the dishes outside the door, he let the door close behind him. He got stuck out in the hallway in nothing but a little pair of briefs. He kept banging on the door, but of course I couldn't hear him from the shower. Poor guy had to go all the way down to the front desk and get another key made. He was so pissed."

I found myself chuckling along to her story, enjoying the fact that I was bonding with the significant other of a fighter. Never mind that it was at the expense of David Grand's dignity. It made me feel like I was part of the culture. I didn't want to be an outsider, always hovering around the edges, pretending to be with Kage in a professional capacity rather than a personal one. I wanted to support him and cheer for him the way my girlfriends had cheered for me when I played sports. I would have bet a million dollars that Farrah ran up and threw her arms around her boyfriend and gave him a big kiss every time he won a fight.

What would it feel like to be recognized as his? For people to whisper, "*That's Michael Kage's boyfriend.*"

"You know, your boss is hot," Farrah said, and I hid my shock behind a fake cough. "Don't get me wrong, I love my boyfriend. But a girl can look, right? You don't just go blind when you're in a committed relationship. And that Michael Kage is something else. All the women are talking about him."

"All the women? What women?" I demanded a little more forcefully than I'd intended.

"You know… the wives and girlfriends, the female fighters, the groupies. Don't you ever read the blog comments? I follow those things religiously. YouTube comments, fan sites, social media stuff. You ought to tell him that. Tell him to go online and look at all the great things people are saying about him. But not the negative stuff. There are lots of haters. Trust me, every fighter has haters, and then they have their stalkers. I'm sure you guys will be figuring this stuff out for yourselves soon enough. In fact, as his assistant you probably ought to keep an eye on that stuff for him. Why don't you go on Twitter right now and follow the UFC?"

On the stage, some of the fighters had begun answering questions. Camera crews were filming. This was a big deal. Kage had not been asked anything yet, so he was just sitting there quietly, taking in every word around him in his calculating way. As for myself, I was pouting over Farrah's words. I loved the fact that people admired Kage. How could they not? What I didn't like was having to bite my tongue.

"Who does Kage's tweets?" Farrah asked.

I shrugged. "I used to do a little bit of social media for him, but he has a PR team working on it now. I have no part of it."

"Well you should at least follow him. And follow the UFC and some of the big blogs. They're all tweeting live about this event. I have my notifications silenced right now, but I see them coming in."

I pulled out my phone and logged on to Twitter. Of course, it was a new phone, so I had to install the app. Social media was pretty much a chore for me, but Farrah was right. I did need to keep an eye on what was being said, at least by the big people who mattered. And I definitely ought to watch what Kage's PR team was saying on his behalf.

"Have you met his fiancée, Vanessa Hale?"

I turned and stared at Farrah, reminding myself that she was a perfectly nice girl, and that it wasn't her fault she didn't know the real deal. She wasn't making me feel like shit on purpose.

"I have indeed met the fabulous Miss Vanessa Hale," I said, using vagueness as a shield. Kage had given me the impression that he wasn't going to play along with the pretend engagement anymore, but we hadn't actually discussed it in depth. I had no idea what his plan was, or how I should handle questions concerning Vanessa.

Farrah pelted me with questions. "Is she as gorgeous in person as she is in the Victoria's Secret catalogs? I heard those girls look anorexic in person, because they have to lose ten extra pounds for the camera. Is that true?"

I sighed. "Actually, Vanessa is awesome. She's got this down-to-earth vibe that's really attractive."

"Is that like saying a girl has a good personality?"

I frowned, not even bothering to hide my confusion. Because how the hell did she get *that* from what I said? "No, it's not like that at all. In my opinion, her looks are even better than her personality. But I may be biased."

"Of course, because you're a guy. I guess that was a stupid question, anyway. Is she coming to the after party they're having when the press conference is over? They're setting it up down the hall in the ballroom." She wagged her eyebrows. "It's gonna be open bar."

"Is that really a good idea? A room full of drunk fighters sounds a little like a 911 call in the making."

"You may have a point." She laughed. "But listen, I know you're on the clock. Your boss keeps looking over here, and I don't want to get you in trouble. Just put it all on me. Tell him I was bugging you."

As she went back to wherever she had come from, I looked up to find Kage watching me. From Farrah's comment, I'd expected him to look stern or angry, but he didn't. He just looked curious, and beautiful in his untamed masculine way.

In the beginning of the conference, the interviewers seemed to be focused mostly on the Lightweight Division, and that was a big yawn for me. I busied myself with the Twitter app, following people, setting up notifications for Kage-related hashtags, reading some of the tweets. The UFC had already tweeted a photo of the fighters sitting on the stage, and the accompanying comment read: *So much testosterone in one room. #ThisIsSparta.*

Finally the interviewers started getting around to the Welterweights, and eventually someone asked Kage a question. I perked up when they called his name. Unfortunately, the question did not have anything to do with fighting, and it pissed me right-the-fuck off.

"So Kage, is it true that you're engaged to Vanessa Hale? Have you two set a date?"

Really? That was the first question he got? I'd already suffered through a Q and A about the girl myself, courtesy of Farrah. Maybe we should have let Vanessa attend the event instead, and then Kage and I could be in a bed somewhere, making up for lost time.

I thought I saw Kage's eyes flick briefly to me before he answered, looking perturbed and guilty all at once. "I'd prefer not to discuss my private life. If you have a question about fighting, I'd be glad to answer that."

"Sure." The reporter changed direction smoothly, firing off an alternate question without even acknowledging that his first had been shot down. "How do you feel about the buzz surrounding you and your quick rise through the ranks? Some people think you're not having to pay your dues like everyone else."

Wow, this reporter just had a knack for asking uncomfortable questions.

Kage smiled at him, an undercurrent of hostility wavering just beneath his expression. "By paying dues, I'm assuming you mean fighting? It may not have been televised with pretty lights and a concession stand, but I assure you I have paid my dues and then some. In fact, there are a couple of guys sitting up here with me right now who know that firsthand, but they're not going to raise their hands and admit they got their asses handed to them by a guy who hasn't paid his dues. So you're just going to have to take my word for it."

"Who do you want to fight next?" another reporter yelled.

Without a second's hesitation, Kage said, "Nick Riker."

Riker's head spun around like he was auditioning for the Exorcist. "Yeah, I bet you would, you arrogant fucker."

And just like that, the tone of the entire event changed. I tensed up, waiting for a fight to break out.

Kage stared calmly at the other fighter, looking every bit the arrogant fucker he'd just been called. "You seem scared, Riker. I heard you were the one screaming the loudest about me not paying my dues. You said I'm not good enough for the contract I got or for the promo the organization's been giving me. I figured you'd want to prove your point. Put me in my place."

Riker's face was red with fury at being called out right in the middle of a huge media event. I couldn't blame him, though I totally wanted Kage to kick his ass.

The reporter yelled, "What's the matter, Riker? You don't want to fight the Machine?" I hadn't expected members of the press to get in on the taunting, but this guy was clearly encouraging an altercation, egging them on like a kid on the playground.

"No, he doesn't." Kage answered before Riker could. "He's not gonna fight me if he can help it, because he's scared. His manager has already been begging the UFC not to make the fight."

"Where did you hear that bullshit?" Riker demanded.

"I have my sources. Doesn't matter. The fight is going to happen, and you're going to lose." Kage gave Riker a wicked grin, and I could have sworn he mouthed the word, "*again.*"

Adrenaline was surging through my veins just watching the exchange, so I couldn't imagine how the two of those guys felt actually taking part in it. This was real. I had no idea Kage could be so ruthless. It turned me on that he could dominate another man so thoroughly without even laying a hand on him.

Kage was damn good at intimidation. Scary good, in fact. If I didn't know him so intimately, it would be easy to believe he was a narcissist, or even a psychopath. He just had that certain look in his eyes.

And then it hit me. The look in his eyes that everybody kept harping about, the one I could never see... I had just witnessed firsthand, and it was chilling.

I'd seen him angry before. When we had our showdown in my parents' backyard, he'd been livid, and it had been directed straight at me. Hell, I'd even seen him murderous before. When he found me in the club that night, on the verge of being double stuffed by those two big guys, I thought he was going to kill someone.

I'd watched him pick apart opponents in the octagon, toying with them like a true predator before defeating them. And I'd seen his beautiful features contort with aggression as he fucked me into oblivion.

What I was watching on the stage of this press conference was something entirely different. There was no emotion there at all, and that's what scared me.

"Fuck this." Riker rose and stalked toward the edge of the stage. "I'm not sticking around for this. Everybody knows this is all a publicity stunt for the UFC's new pet, and they're not paying me enough to play along. I'm going to see if they've opened the bar yet."

I sat in stunned silence, wondering if what he'd said was true, or if he was just scared like Kage had said. It was possible that this was all a publicity stunt. It was even possible that Riker's temper tantrum and angry exit was part of it. I remembered what Kage had said over the phone when he'd told me about the event. Were they really trying to bring in some of the drama of pro wrestling?

I'd watched pro wrestling some as a child, and I remembered the theatrics involved. Outside the ring, the wrestlers had engaged in on-camera stories that put the soap operas to shame: fights, arguments, vendettas. And then when the women joined the show, they added affairs, cheating, jealousy, and love triangles. But the fighting itself was fake, or what those in the business called *work*. Kage had said they wanted to keep MMA real, so that was reassuring. I couldn't imagine him faking a fight for any amount of money. Hell, I doubted if he could hold back enough to do it. That man loved to fight, and he loved to win.

My phone vibrated with a notification, and I saw that someone had tweeted about what had just happened on the stage. *"OMG Kage just called out Riker. #HolyShit #WelcomeToTheMachine."*

"Enjoying the show?" The smooth voice brought my arm hairs to attention. Peter Santori lowered himself into the chair Farrah had vacated, keeping his eyes trained on the stage as if I were too insignificant to bother looking at. His charcoal suit was so perfectly fitted, it was like an extension of the man himself.

I allowed my eyes to roam freely over his handsome face. He was an older, polished version of his nephew, with deep green eyes, unblemished skin, and a strategically stubbled jaw. The similarity between the two men was as unsettling as it was mesmerizing.

"Uh… Yes, sir," I finally managed to say, wishing I could have said something less submissive. Damn his superiority. This was the psycho who was having me watched, and who was controlling the man I loved. I hated him, yet I called him sir. I instinctively showed the man respect, even when I knew he didn't deserve it.

"I'm surprised you're still hanging around," he said. "We've hired a real PR firm to handle Michael's public image. There's really no reason for you to keep trying to insert yourself where you're not wanted."

"Kage invited me." My simple, childlike answer infuriated me, because it was all I had. I felt unarmed against him.

"Yes, I imagine he did. He loves to rebel against me, you know. Always has. If he thinks I won't like it, he makes it a point to do it. So of course the minute I told him I didn't approve of you as a publicist, he went overboard to get you as involved in his career and his life as he possibly could. If I could stop pushing the issue, he would get bored and move on. The problem, as I'm sure you've noticed, is that the Santori's have a stubborn streak. We each want to force our will on the other. It's a fault."

I glanced up at the stage, hoping for moral support from Kage. His eyes were focused dead on Santori, and the contempt within them was unmistakable. In fact, the two of them were staring at each other like animals, and I was just a scrap of meat.

Then Santori smiled at him and held up his hands in mock surrender. I was pretty sure he didn't mean it.

He turned to face me for the first time since he'd sat down. The smile still ghosted his lips, but his eyes were untouched. "You break up with Michael, or I'll disown him. Do you hear me? He'll have nothing, and it will be all your fault. I could also put in a call to your professor, and one to the dean of your school. Sexual misconduct is an embarrassing blemish to have on your record."

"Do you speak from experience?" The comment was stupid. I guess my inner smartass didn't give a damn who Santori was, or that he would not hesitate to smash my hopes and dreams. And possibly my ankles.

He kept his cool, though, as he stood and walked away. The man was nothing if not controlled. I thought again how much Kage resembled him, both in appearance and in demeanor. But Kage had that rough-edged quality that made him more human than Santori. He was a big, rough teddy bear, and right now I just wanted to curl up against his chest and let him wrap me up in those muscled arms. I couldn't imagine his uncle ever holding that kind of appeal for anyone. He was handsome, but there was no humanity there. Peter Santori was more a machine than his nephew would ever be.

8

(JAMIE)

THE AFTER PARTY, as Farrah had called it, was more like a bad wedding reception to me. There were tables filled with fancy nibbles, a DJ playing overly-suggestive dance music, and the infamous open bar that seemed to be on everyone's mind. My opinion had not changed concerning the intelligence of throwing a bunch of drunk fighters together in a room. I was convinced nothing good could come of it.

Kage texted me to say he would see me at the party, but that he'd been asked to meet with some people from the organization. It was business, so I couldn't argue.

"*I won't be long,*" he texted. "*But you tell me if Santori comes back, and I'll be there in a heartbeat.*"

"*I'll be fine, Daddy,*" I fired back, trying to disguise my unease.

"*Don't be mean.*"

"*I'm not. I'm being sexy.*" I tacked on a winky face.

"*In that case, call me Big Daddy.*"

"*Haha. You might have to refresh my memory on the BIG part. It's been a while.*"

"*Oops. Gotta go.*"

And then I was alone at the reception, and that open bar was looking mighty tempting. I made my way over to it and ordered a Jack and Coke, and then I wandered around trying to act less awkward than I felt. Nothing strange about being the only person in the room who wasn't engaged in conversation or at least standing beside someone. Especially when the lights turned down low, and it started seeming like a real party.

After about fifteen minutes, Farrah saved me. She hopped up beside me and gave me the kind of smile that said she'd probably already paid a couple of visits to the bar.

"Hello Jamie Atwood, *Assistant.*"

I smiled, surprised she'd remembered my name. "Hello Farrah, *Girlfriend of David.*"

She liked that a lot. I could tell by the way she latched onto my arm and giggled. "So where is your boss man?"

"He's in a meeting of some kind. He'll be out soon."

"Oooh, a meeting. That's interesting."

"Where's your boyfriend?" I glanced pointedly at her hand on my arm. "Probably about to beat my ass, right?"

"Oh, sorry. I get touchy-feely with everyone when I've been drinking."

"It's okay." Of course I didn't tell her I was just as concerned about *my* boyfriend seeing it as I was hers.

Another girl wandered up, dressed and pierced similarly to Farrah. "There you are," she slurred. "I was about to go looking for you in the parking lot."

Farrah hung on her arm just like she had mine, confirming that she did indeed get touchy-feely when she'd been drinking. "I'm talking to Michael Kage's assistant. He says Kage is in a meeting, so I'm assuming he's in the same one with David. Maybe they're going to fight each other."

"You think?" I wondered if that would mean that Farrah and I couldn't be friends anymore. I was disappointed at the thought, since Farrah was the first friend I'd made on my own in the UFC universe. Meeting her helped to ground me, even if she had no idea just how similar she and I were.

"Would you like to dance with me?" Farrah's friend gazed hopefully at me with big blue eyes.

"I don't think this is that kind of party," I began, but one glance out over the crowd revealed that people had moved to the dance floor and started dancing. "Oh, I guess it is. But no, thanks. I'd better not."

"Are you still on the clock?" Farrah poked out her bottom lip before taking a swig of whatever she was drinking.

"I'm always on the clock, girls. Michael Kage is very demanding, so I have to be ready to do whatever he wants at a moment's notice."

"So does that mean you don't want to dance?" the friend asked.

"I'm afraid so. Besides, I'm not a great dancer."

I checked my phone again for lack of anything better to do. The event had generated a substantial buzz, so I had to skim a lot of tweets that didn't interest me. Someone had posted a picture of a red-faced Riker storming off the stage. Kage appeared calm and calculating in the background as the other man visibly lost his composure.

Some asshole commented, *"He's got a point. Kage hasn't fought anybody yet. #PayYourDues #TeamRiker,"* which inspired the reply, *"Riker is a pussy. I predict Kage will submit him in round 1. #TeamKage #RearNakedChoke."* When some girl chimed in with, *"Kage is hot. #TeamKage #ManCrushMonday,"* that was my cue to put my phone away.

"You're following it now, huh?" Farrah asked, smiling as proudly as if she'd actually invented social media. "It's addictive. Trust me, I'm on there all the time. I have to put my phone on airplane mode when the temptation gets too strong."

The friend sighed and took a swallow of her drink. "You know a party is lame when stalking Twitter is more fun. I thought this would be like a celebrity thing, you know? I haven't even seen the Octagon Girls. I should have gone to that frat party instead. "

"You're probably safer here" I said. "At least here you won't have guys posting naked pictures of you after you pass out."

"We hope," Farrah added. "Some of the guys are already pretty trashed."

A quick scan of the room revealed that some of the attendees definitely seemed loose, which made me thirsty. "I'm going to get another drink, girls."

They walked with me to the bar, where we all got refills. Thirty minutes later, I was draining my third Jack and Coke, and our little group had expanded to include me and six others— all girls. They were a rapt audience as I explained exactly what being a journalism major entailed, and apparently it was a pretty funny subject, because I was bringing down the house when Kage walked up.

"Looks like you're having a good time," he said with a grin, wading through girls to get to me.

I raised my empty glass in salute. "That we are, Big Daddy."

Several girls giggled, and Kage's eyebrows flew up. "How much have you had to drink, Jamie?"

"Just enough, I think."

He nodded. "Guess I need to play catch-up. Walk with me to the bar?"

I followed, and so did my entourage.

Farrah tapped Kage on the shoulder, and I think I saw her wince when he turned his shrewd gaze toward her. "Sorry to interrupt, but have you seen David Grand? He's my boyfriend."

"Yeah, I saw him head toward the restrooms."

She took off to find her missing boyfriend without another word to any of us.

"So I see you've made some new friends." He downed a double shot of tequila and set the glass down on the bar. "That's nice. I was worried you'd be lonely."

"Nope. I'm very popular with the UFC crowd. Lots of people want to be friends with Michael Kage's assistant."

"I'm sure they do. I couldn't help but notice they're all of the female persuasion."

"What about it?" I leaned over to get the bartender's attention for another drink, but Kage grabbed me by the arm and pulled me back. I scowled at him. "Why won't you let me get another drink? I'm thirsty."

"I think you've probably had enough. Don't get me wrong. You're adorable when you're drunk, but I've got plans for tonight that don't include you being unconscious."

"Fine," I huffed. "But I'm not drunk. I only had three drinks, and I'm just barely feeling it."

"Well, something's up with you. Are you upset? I know my uncle accosted you earlier, and we need to discuss that when we can get some privacy."

"There's nothing to discuss. He basically told me to fuck off or he'd call the school and report me for—" I glanced around to make sure no one was listening, then whispered, "sexual misconduct."

I saw a wave of intense anger ripple across Kage's features, and then it was gone, pushed down to wherever it was he pushed those feelings that were too inconvenient to deal with. He seemed to do it a lot where his uncle was concerned. He leaned in close enough to speak against my ear. "Don't worry, baby. I'll take care of you."

"Will you? I don't know, I'm beginning to think it's just a permanent part of what I signed on for. Am I gonna have to worry about this when I graduate? When I go for my first job interview?

128

Oh, don't mind those men in black. They're just some thugs Kage's crazy uncle hired to watch every fucking move I make."

"Yeah, you've had too much to drink. We probably ought to call it a night." He took me gently by the arm and led me toward the exit doors, but before we could get there, we discovered a surprise guest wandering around looking for Kage.

Vanessa Hale. Fuck.

She smiled brightly at Kage, but her pretty features drew tight as soon as she saw me. "Mikey… Jamie, I didn't expect to see you here."

"Likewise." I didn't even try to smile, because she looked way too good in her little black dress. She had that effortless kind of beauty, with barely there makeup and long brown hair that fell in waves over one shoulder. The freckles and subtle gap between her front teeth set her apart from the clones who dominate the modeling industry. I loved her and hated her at the same time.

"Hi, Nessy." Kage took her arm in his other hand and ushered the two of us to an empty table as far away from other people as possible. "What are you doing here? We were just leaving."

Vanessa looked confused. "I was told by your PR team that you wanted me to do a publicity thing. That there would be reporters and photographers here."

"There are," Kage said. "But I was actually trying to avoid them. As far as I'm concerned, they got enough pictures of me during the press conference."

"Oh." Vanessa chewed at her lip. "When I was walking around the party looking for you, I may have told one of the photographers that he could get some shots of us together. I'm sorry, Kage. I had no idea you didn't want to do it, so when he asked, I said yes."

"Dammit." Kage took a deep breath and looked at the ceiling, deep in thought as he tried to figure out how to handle the new development. "I just want to go home."

"So I guess that means no hanging out with the other fighters and their significant others?"

Kage snorted. "You know me. Do you think I want to go chat with the other fighters? Besides, I'm the shark in their midst right now. They hate my fucking guts."

I couldn't help being impressed. "Are you becoming infamous?"

"Baby, I've always been infamous. I've just taken it to prime time now."

"There's the ego we know and love," Vanessa said absently, running one of her midnight blue nails along her lip. "Jamie, why don't you come walk around with me for just a minute? I wanted to look at some of these people up close, and I don't want to go alone."

Kage answered for me. "Jamie's not going anywhere. He's had too much to drink, and I need to take him home."

"I have not had too much to drink," I insisted. "I'm just wired, that's all. I had that messed up conversation with Uncle You-know-who, and then I had to wait forever for you to come out of that top secret meeting. And no offense, Vanessa... I understand why this whole publicity thing with you two is going on, but if I have to hear one more girl gushing to me about how lucky you are to be engaged to my boyfriend, I'm gonna lose my shit. I'm not built to handle all of this espionage and double-dealing."

"You might want to rethink your choice of boyfriend, then," Vanessa said. "Mikey and Santori are a package deal. The man may not come around much, but his shadow will always be over everything you do."

Kage frowned. "Way to try to scare him off, Vanessa."

"It's true. You've always had to live with it, so it's normal to you. Which is not healthy, by the way."

"What do you expect me to do? My entire life is wrapped up in that hotel. Everything I have, everything I'll ever be."

I reached under the table and touched his hand, getting his attention and calming him down. "What about this UFC contract? I thought that was your future."

He laughed. "Jamie, that's my dream— the goal that I've always been after since I was a little kid. But I'm Santori's sole heir. The Alcazar will be mine one day."

"I thought you weren't that concerned about money."

He smiled indulgently at me. "It's easy to not be concerned about money when you've got plenty of it. But it's more complicated than that. The Alcazar is my home. It's part of who I am."

There was a triumphant gleam in Vanessa's eyes. "See, I told you, Jamie. I think the two of you make a great couple, but you've got to realize what you're getting when you take on this big lug. He's never going to be free of his uncle. Not until Santori dies, and at his age, I'm betting he's got at least thirty years. Probably more like forty. People who are that mean don't die young. They hang around until they've made everyone thoroughly miserable."

"Has Santori done stuff to you?" I asked Vanessa. "Has he threatened you or caused you problems?"

"No, but I've seen what he's done to Mikey over the years, and it breaks my heart."

Kage snorted. "You make me sound helpless. I assure you I am not helpless."

"Where Santori is concerned, you are. I love you, Mikey. You're the strongest, most confident guy I know, but that man is your kryptonite." She reached across him and pinched my cheek. "And this pretty thing is running a close second."

"What?" I batted her hand away. "I'm nothing like Santori. Don't even play like that."

"I didn't say you were like him. I just meant that you're a weakness." She laughed. "Stop pouting. If that lip drags any lower it'll touch the floor."

Kage rested a hand on my thigh and leaned in to whisper against my ear. "She's right, you know. You're definitely a weakness." He latched onto my earlobe and sucked it, making my entire body shudder, and then he was gone and sitting upright again as if it had never happened.

Vanessa groaned. "You are so damn obvious. I hope you know what you're doing, because it's only a matter of time before people start noticing how you are around him. Then everybody will be talking about it, and your uncle will kill both of you, and then I'll be out of a perfectly good beard job."

She was joking about the killing part, but it made me uneasy just the same. She'd never had Santori on her ass like he was on mine. The guy was seriously creeping me out with his veiled threats and dead eyes.

Eyes that looked like Kage's.

I shuddered again, and this time it was not from desire.

"If I come out, Santori won't have any reason to threaten us anymore," Kage said. "That's why I'm seriously considering doing it. He doesn't give a damn who I date. All he cares about is me fulfilling the plan he's laid out for me, which is becoming a UFC champion. If I can come out, keep my contract, *and* earn a title, Santori will see that his concern was all for nothing. Then I won't have to give up everything."

Vanessa shook her head. "You're playing with fire, Mikey. What if you're wrong?"

"What choice do I have? Keep letting him control every move I make? Give Jamie up and be alone?"

"I don't know. It's all too complicated to think about." She stood up and kissed him on top of the head. "I'm going to get a drink and mingle. You let me know what you decide about the publicity stuff and our fake wedding. Is there such a thing as a fake wedding planner?"

Kage laughed. "Shut up."

Vanessa made her way through the crowd to the bar, and I was more than glad to have Kage all to myself again. Still thinking about his mouth on my earlobe, remembering all too well the warmth and the wetness and the gentle scrape of his teeth, I reached under the table again. This time I bypassed his hand and went straight for his dick.

He licked his lips and pushed his hips subtly toward my hand. "I want to jump you so bad right now."

"I know. All this pretending is really starting to take a toll on me. How long will we have to be like this?"

He smiled, looking almost shy. "A title shot may happen sooner than we thought. That's what we discussed in that top secret meeting you were bitching about. I'm going to fight David Grand next, and then the winner of that fight gets a shot at Nick Riker's belt."

"Oh my God, that is fantastic!"

"Yeah." Kage watched me closely as I pulled away from him and settled back into my seat. The way he tracked me with his eyes, I could tell I was a hundred percent on his sex radar at that moment. His mouth was talking, but his eyes were already back at the hotel undressing me. "Riker and Grand aren't crazy about the plan. I can't blame them, really. Just between us, they're absolutely right about the whole thing. I haven't actually paid my dues in the official UFC octagon."

"I don't see why that matters. It's just a technicality. Everyone knows you're going to kick their asses."

"That's the point. They know they're not going to get to keep their places much longer, because I'm gunning for them. If I was fighting my way up through the ranks, there would be other fights to slow me down, more chances to fuck up and get a loss on my record. The guys at the top would have some time before I got to them. This way, they know they've each probably got one more fight before they drop in rank. Riker will lose his title, and Grand will probably lose his shot at ever winning it at all. It sucks for them, but I can't help that. I'm not going to sacrifice my dream so that they can have theirs."

"How quickly do you think this all could happen?"

"Maybe as soon as six months. Possibly a little longer."

"So in less than a year, I'll be a college graduate, and you could be the Welterweight Champion. That would mean…" I didn't know how to finish my thought. The feelings I was having seemed too fast, too serious. He might laugh at me or back off if I dared to give voice to those thoughts.

Chapter

9

(KAGE)

W E COULD BE together for real." I finished Jamie's thought for him, because I knew he wouldn't.

When it came to expressing our feelings for each other, we had an odd dynamic. He'd already told me he loved me, but I had yet to say the words. On the other hand, I was much more willing to talk about our future together, while he danced around it like it was an illusion that would shatter into a million pieces if he dared to acknowledge it.

At least he was willing enough to acknowledge the sex part of it. He'd been bolder lately, making more overtures toward me. The way he'd goaded me into fucking him in the pantry at his parents' house still blew my mind every time I thought about it. And believe me, I thought about it a *lot*. It was surprising how much I liked it when he got aggressive, because aggressiveness had never been a trait I wanted in a lover. With Jamie, it was different. When he came after me, it was proof that the attraction was just as strong from his side as it was from mine.

The after party was pure torture. Did they really expect me to play nice with these guys? All I wanted to do was bash their heads in and take their spots. When I looked at them, I didn't see a colleague or teammate or peer. I saw an opportunity. There was one exception to that rule: Jason Kinney. It looked like he had a good shot at a UFC contract in the near future, especially since I had my foot in the door now, and he was the closest thing to a teammate I'd ever had. I didn't relish the thought of having to face him in the octagon.

"Let's get out of here," I told Jamie. "I'm tired of thinking about fighting. All I want to do is get you home, lock the door, and stay in all weekend. No training, no homework, no business or school whatsoever."

"Sounds good to me." He stood up, and I followed. I called Aldo on the way out and told him to come get us.

When I got off the phone, Jamie had his cell out and was devouring tweets. "Since when are you one of those people who walks around with your nose buried in a phone?"

Without looking up, he answered, "Since people are talking about you and what's going on at this press conference."

"I can only imagine what they're saying."

"Some are praising you like you're their new god, others are denouncing you as Satan. The usual social-media crap. One person says something, and the next person has to say the opposite. Oh, and they want your girlfriend, of course. Well, the guys do. All the girls want to *be* your girlfriend, and have your babies. That was mentioned. *#MachineBabies*."

"Jamie get off of that phone. You don't need to obsess over that bullshit. Just like you said, it's all the same. People enjoy arguing for the sake of arguing."

"But you can find out what people think of you," he said.

"I don't care what people think of me. If I win a fight, that speaks for itself. It doesn't matter if anyone *thinks* I'm going to win, or if they think I deserve to win. Action is all that matters, and the rest is just spinning wheels."

He didn't put his phone away, though. Not even when the limo pulled up to the curb and we climbed into the backseat. As usual, Aldo was driving, and Aaron was riding shotgun.

"Where's Miss Hale?" Aldo craned his neck to get a clear view of the hotel entrance, presumably to see if Vanessa was schlepping along behind us. "We drove her over here tonight. Is she not ready to go?"

"It's just us boys tonight, Aldo. Vanessa can take care of herself."

Aldo scoffed. "I think maybe she needs me to take care of her. You tell her that. Tell her there's a real man here who knows what to do with her."

"Tell her yourself, Aldo. I've got enough of my own shit to deal with."

"You've got that right," Jamie groaned. "Kage, this is not good. You need to look at this tweet."

"I told you I don't care what they think of me."

He shoved the phone in front of my face anyway, forcing me to look at a photo that had been uploaded of us sitting at the table with Vanessa. Someone had snapped the picture at the exact moment when I'd leaned over to whisper in Jamie's ear, taking that naughty little detour to suck his earlobe into my mouth. Vanessa sat beside me rolling her eyes. It was so quick, barely a second in time, and yet some enterprising blogger had managed to capture my indiscretion for the whole world to see.

It got a little hard to breathe then. For all my big talk about coming out and not caring what people thought, seeing that photo posted up in public like that really spun me out. Because, dammit, this wasn't the way it was supposed to happen. I wasn't ready. Vanessa's warning came back to me, and I closed my eyes and took a deep breath. I wasn't ready. *I'm not ready.*

"It's not that obvious, Kage," Jamie said. "Yeah, your face is all shoved up into the side of mine, but it's not exactly obvious that my earlobe is actually *inside* your mouth. It could be a trick of the lighting. Or a joke. You know, like a prank."

"Are you Braden now?" I grinned, because what else could I do? Hell, I'd been flirting with getting found out since Jamie stood in front of me that first night in Atlanta. I'd known even then he'd be my undoing, and I'd been clamoring to get undone ever since. I'd pushed and taken chances even when everyone else, including Jamie, was trying to warn me. Now was the day of reckoning, and I was just going to have to man up and admit that it was all my fault.

Jamie kept reading his phone, his eyes going wide. "Oh, God. Someone tweeted, '*Looks like Victoria's not the only one who has a secret. #gay.*'"

"Jamie, put the phone away."

"Only a few people are making gay comments, though. Most of them are saying it's a joke. One of them pointed out that Vanessa is sitting right there beside you and rolling her eyes, so it's obviously a joke."

"Obviously. Put the phone away."

"This one is a guy. He says, *'You can choke me anytime, daddy. #gasper'* Apparently he doesn't mind if you're gay."

Instead of ordering Jamie to put the phone away, I took it from him. He made a whimper and nearly lunged for it, but I tossed it onto the seat beside me. Then I grabbed him and pulled him onto my lap, facing me, and positioned his thighs on either side of mine so that he was riding my legs.

"What's a gasper?" he asked, and I had to shake my head at his innocence.

"That stuff is not real," I told him. "It's just noise. What we have between us is real. You can't let that noise interfere with this, okay? We've got enough people trying to tell us we can't be together, or putting rules on when or where we can be together. My uncle says we can never be together because it will destroy my career. Your parents say we can be together, but not under their roof unless we're married. There's constantly someone calling us down and telling us we're taking risks, or telling us not to show affection in front of them even though they do it in front of us. It's all bullshit."

Jamie leaned in to me, and I took his mouth in a kiss. His lips were so soft and plump, made just for me to suck and abuse. I worked them apart with the tip of my tongue, licking into his mouth and tasting the bite of whisky. He opened up, and everything faded away until there was only him and me and the subtle hum of the engine as we moved through the city. And then Aldo had to go and ruin it.

"Hey could you two knock it off back there? Nobody wants to see whatever kinky shit you guys get up to." I didn't point out that Aaron had turned half around in his seat and was glancing into the backseat often enough to call it watching.

"Fuck you, Aldo. You should be used to seeing it by now with all the spying my uncle has you doing."

"Hey, I don't do no grunt work," he said. "You'll have to take that up with somebody else."

"So no X-rated films starring the two of us have made it into your hands? Is that what you're telling me?"

"I ain't telling you nothing. But I will give you a word of advice. Conduct yourself properly, and nobody has a reason to mess with you. That's something you never could understand."

"I haven't done anything wrong, Aldo. I just want to live my life."

"Your life ain't really yours to live, kid. Never was." He laughed. "Hell, mine ain't either. You know that."

"You may be right, Aldo. Maybe my life hasn't been my own up until now, but I'm done living for someone else. For the first step, I had someone sweep my apartment for surveillance equipment. It's all gone now, and it had better stay gone. No more spying on me, and no more Kage and Jamie porn— though I would actually like a copy of anything you already have. Especially that first one."

Aaron squirmed in the passenger seat, and Aldo grunted.

During my argument with Aldo, Jamie had curled up against my chest and gone still. I knew he wasn't asleep, because his breathing wasn't steady enough for that. But he was content, and it felt good to hold him close.

STEVE greeted us when we entered the Alcazar.

"What are you doing working night shift?" I asked, noting his unusually unkempt appearance and weary eyes.

He yawned. "Filling in. I'm pulling a double, and I am not fucking happy about it. I hope they fire the girl who's supposed to be working this shift, because she didn't even bother calling in. Now I'm missing a hot date with a member of that wedding party that checked in yesterday. He's a fireman, Kage.... A fireman. And if I don't get a do-over on that date, I'll kill that lazy bitch myself."

"Nice to see you, too, Steve." Jamie walked around behind the desk to give the stressed-out clerk a hug.

"I'm sorry, Jamie. I'm just not in the best mood right now." He ruffled Jamie's hair and smiled. "It is good to see you again, though. I expect to see even more of you after you graduate."

I couldn't help smiling when Jamie turned shy. "Oh, I don't know what I'll be doing."

"I do." I reached out and latched onto his arm. "We have to go upstairs now, Steve."

"Of course." Steve leaned his elbows on the counter and let out a bored sigh. "If you see a cute fireman wandering around up there, tell him I'm down here all by my lonesome with nothing to do."

Once we were on the elevator, I moved in front of Jamie and leered down at him. "We're almost home again. Have you missed it?"

"More than I want to admit. Who could have imagined that a summer job would turn into... this?"

"This," I repeated. "You know, Steve just got me thinking with that comment about seeing more of you after graduation. We haven't really discussed what we're going to do."

"What do you want to do?" he asked uncertainly, not meeting my gaze.

"I want you to pack all of your shit in the Range Rover and drive up here. Then I want you to park it in one of the two parking spaces designated for this apartment. I'll help you bring your things up, and we'll put them in the drawers and the closet in the master bedroom. Then we'll just live. How does that sound?"

He laughed as the elevator came to a stop, and the doors slid open. "So you've only worked out the plan for one day?"

"Do we need more?" I used my key card to open the door to my apartment, and we stepped inside. "Actually, I do have one more day planned. Because we're going to have to go visit your family at some point in the future, and I'm not going to sleep in separate beds, so that means we'll have to get married. That takes care of another day."

He laughed even harder this time. "Was that meant to be a proposal or something? Because I was under the impression that you were supposed to get down on one knee."

I started pinging the buttons of his dress shirt, making quick work of the top five and then ripping both the shirt and undershirt over his head in one smooth move. "I'm not that romantic," I pointed out. "And you're the only one who's getting on his knees."

"You are so fucking cocky. Why don't you get on your knees?"

"Hmmm. No. I want you completely naked on your knees. Now get stripping."

He did exactly what I told him to, because he got off on it just like I did. "*Make me*," he'd said when we were sitting in Atlanta traffic and I'd told him to suck my dick. And that's exactly what he wanted. Every time I got forceful with him, his eyes would go all soft and wanting, like they were just pleading with me to *make him*.

"Now get on your knees." He dropped to his knees in the middle of the living room floor, and I unzipped my fly. I liked this dynamic. Him naked and vulnerable while I was fully dressed and looking down at him. It turned me on not because I enjoyed bullying him into submission, but because he was mine, and he wanted to please me.

Just then a knock sounded on my door, and I wanted to hurt whoever was on the other side. Jamie was beautiful and needy on his knees, and my cock was already out. *Fuck.* But no one ever knocked on my door.

"Get over there," I hissed, pointing at the sofa. "Grab the blanket and cover yourself." I stuffed my dick back into my pants with an annoyed growl and answered the door.

"Santori," I gasped. "What are you doing here?"

"I need to speak to you now, Michael." He glanced over my shoulder at Jamie, who was huddled under the blanket on the sofa. "In my apartment."

"I'll be right back, baby," I told Jamie before I followed Santori down the hall.

The man didn't waste any time getting down to business. "Do you have any idea what kind of a spectacle you made of yourself at that event tonight?" he demanded. "Why did you have to bring him along? If you absolutely must have him, at least keep him hidden away. For heaven's sake, do you have no sense at all of self-preservation?"

I sighed, so damn weary of this same argument I kept having to go through, it seemed with every-fucking-body on the planet.

"God, why can't people just mind their own damn business?" I shouted. "Why does anybody care who I'm sleeping with? I don't want Vanessa. I don't want a woman. I don't even want another man. I want Jamie, and that's not going to change. It has nothing to do with whether or not I can fight. I can beat anybody, and I'm *going* to beat everybody in the UFC. I'm going to tear the fucking house down over there. By the time I'm through with them, there won't be a single one of them who will dare step into the octagon with me. So why does it matter if I'm in love with a man?"

"It's just not the way people of quality behave."

"People of quality? Why do you talk that way, like some pretentious asshole? You can drop the proper act around me, Santori. We both know you're no better than a street thug. No better than my father."

"Well, now that's where you're wrong. Your father's problem was that he lacked the Santori blood. We shared a mother, but where my father was a strong man of character and ability who built a good life for his family, Bobby's father was a lowlife piece of garbage who couldn't stay out of prison long enough to keep food on the table for his wife and child. Our mother was lucky to get out when she did. I felt sympathy for your father, of course. But Bobby was much older than me, and already out of control by the time our mother married my father. He stayed in trouble, just like his father. Spent enough time in juvenile detention centers and prison that he forgot how to be civilized. There was really no hope for him. I didn't want that to be your fate, Michael."

"You're lying." I paced across the room and back, my shoulders beginning to tremble with anger. "I know you're lying, because they wouldn't have let him in the Army if he had a criminal record."

"Army?" Santori snorted. "What the hell makes you think he was in the Army?"

"He had the blankets and the food rations. And he always wore that camouflage jacket. I may not know much about my father, but I know that."

The laugh that came out of Santori was cruel, and I knew before he even spoke that what he said was going to hurt. I just didn't know how much.

"That's why you got an eagle in your tattoo isn't it?"

When I didn't answer, he continued. "I thought so. Boy, you went and got a permanent tattoo in honor of something that never was. Your deadbeat father couldn't even hold down a job, much less fight for his country. I don't know about all of the other stuff, but I do know he got the jacket from the Goodwill, so I'm guessing maybe he got all of it there. He sure as hell didn't work for it."

"Shut up," I growled, feeling the anger starting to trump the hurt. "I won't stand here and listen to you berate my father anymore."

He laughed. "Such loyalty to a man who left you. He didn't even love you enough to tell you goodbye. Just disappeared and left you to deal with the death of your brother all alone. And who took care of you? I did. Where is my loyalty?"

"Take your loyalty and shove it up your ass." I stormed out, so angry I was shaking. I looked down at the tattoo on my arm and the eagle so carefully crafted within the collage of objects I had once considered sacred. Now Santori had reduced them to nothing. Just like he did to everything. Just like he did to me.

Dammit, I couldn't go in to see Jamie like this. I was a mess. I needed to just calm the hell down. Deep breaths, deep breaths. I closed my eyes and breathed, and after a few minutes, I was able to enter the apartment.

(JAMIE)

I WAS SITTING on the sofa reading tweets again. I knew I shouldn't have done it after Kage had been so adamant in the limo, but I'd gotten nervous while he was gone with Santori. I'd felt so alone, wondering what they were talking about, knowing it was probably me.

Whether he wanted to admit it, Kage was in trouble, and it was because of me. Maybe it wasn't my fault exactly, but if he'd never met me, he would have been clicking along right on track in his new UFC career. He probably wouldn't even need the distraction of Vanessa, because there would be no real relationship to try to hide. I wouldn't let myself entertain the notion that if it hadn't been me it would have been someone else. It was just too horrible to imagine Kage dating someone else, having sex with someone else, getting photographed in public with someone else. No, if anyone was going to be inspiring gay hashtags with him, I wanted it to be me.

I kept going back to that one message, though. The one about choking. I don't know what it was about it, but somehow it had me fascinated. And jealous. How could I be jealous of a random suggestion made by someone I'd never met? Hell, someone Kage had never even met as far as I knew.

I'd known without asking what the guy was talking about, though. Even when I'd asked Kage what a gasper was, I knew instinctively what it was. So when I had scrolled through all of the tweets I hadn't read, I opened up my internet browser and Googled the word.

Three clicks and a lot of blushing later, Kage came back into the apartment. His face was intense, and even though he gave me what he tried to pass off as a casual greeting, I knew something was wrong. But then wasn't it always when his uncle was involved?

"What are you doing?" he asked. "Reading those comments again?"

"Sort of." In my mind, I didn't know what he would think was worse, the comments or the studying up on the kinky practice of getting off by being choked.

He peered over my shoulder and groaned. "God, Jamie. What are you looking at that for? Are you wanting to try it or something?"

"Not really." I closed my browser and looked guiltily up at him. "Have you ever done it?"

"No." He ran a hand through his hair and growled. "Yes. Some people like that shit."

"And you don't?"

"It's just one of those things, you know? I've never done it unless someone specifically asked me for it, and that was only a couple of times. It's risky, especially when you add sex into the mix— people get carried away. I know what I'm doing, but one wrong move and I could wind up in prison."

He grabbed me by the hand and pulled me to my feet. Then he led me into the bedroom, still naked and still partially aroused. I was getting more aroused by the second knowing he was about to have his way with me.

Pushing me roughly down onto the bed, he got undressed and grabbed the lube. Then he climbed up between my legs, pushing my knees back hard so they were nearly at my shoulders, exposing me so thoroughly it almost made me shy. He dribbled the lube all over my hole and started fingering me open and getting me stretched out. His eyes locked onto mine, the dark determination in them communicating he had only one intention, and that was fucking me.

Then he smacked my ass hard with the flat of his palm. The loud crack rang out into the room, followed up by my surprised cry. There was no lead up with gentle touches, no working up from lighter blows. At least from my end, it felt like he'd skipped all the way to hard as fuck, but then I had no idea just how hard the man could hit. My ass was stinging and aching from the blow, and it only made my cock stiffen and my balls tighten up.

"Do the other side," I said. "Make it even."

He smiled and smacked my other cheek, and I cried out again. This time the sound faded into a low moan of pleasure. Now both of my cheeks were stinging, and I was aching to have him inside me.

His cock was rock hard, leading the way as he pushed in. With my legs flipped so far back toward my ears, the stretch on my hole was mind boggling. Painful and pleasurable at once, an echo of our entire relationship dynamic.

Instead of using his hips to move his cock in and out of me, he rested his hands on the backs of my thighs and rocked me back and forth on the bed. His eyes ate up every detail.

He kept it up until I thought I would die from my building orgasm, and from the way my chest was compressed beneath my legs. It was hard to breathe. But being compromised by him, physically taxed for his pleasure, was what I seemed to live for.

"So fucking tight," he said. "Too bad you can't see this, baby— the way your ass is gripping me. It's taking every bit of control I have to keep from exploding in you right now."

"You can come," I gasped, straining for breath. "I'm close, too."

"I'm not quite ready." He turned me onto my side and climbed onto the bed behind me, slamming his dick back up inside me again and fucking me with a series of hard, fast strokes that left me panting.

Then his arm went around my throat just like when he'd choked me unconscious that day in the gym, and I knew what was about to happen. He didn't squeeze, though. He simply got into position and fucked me, teasing me with the knowledge that I was about to experience the taboo thing that I'd been obsessing over all night. My stomach bottomed out with a mixture of excitement and fear, and I realized I'd probably never be able to watch a rear naked choke again without getting hard.

Kage kept moving inside me, but now his cock head glanced off of my prostate at just the right angle to make a senseless animal out of me. "Is this what you want?" He latched onto my ear and bit down gently, then sucked it into his mouth.

I nodded frantically. "But you don't have to. The risk."

"I love you, Jamie," he growled against my ear. "I'll do anything for you."

"Oh, God. I love you, too." I grabbed onto my aching cock, so close to blowing…so fucking close I could scream.

"Tell me when you're about to—"

"Now," I rasped, feeling my orgasm boiling up from the base of my cock. "I'm coming now."

He squeezed his bent elbow more snugly against my throat in a tight V, the gentle but consistent pressure slowing the blood flow to my sex-addled brain. The sound of his harsh breaths at my ear became a distant sawing, more of a memory really, as cold heat sizzled through my cock, up and out and *oh, God*. There was a tightening, a pulsing, and a delicious warmth that moved like time-lapse clouds across my mind.

Then I was swimming up toward consciousness, watching through closed eyes as tiny bubbles floated and swirled around my head. Kage's face wavered slowly into focus, upside-down, watching me closely from above.

"Welcome back," he said with a smile.

I started, realizing that my last coherent memory had been of shooting all over myself. I looked down at my body, and for a second I felt shame. My dick was softening against my belly, and I was splattered with droplets of my own semen. Kage lifted my head from his thighs and slipped out from under me, crawling around to look down at me properly. He planted a soft kiss on my lips.

"I—"

When he didn't finish his sentence, I prompted, "You what?"

"I… was just wondering how that felt."

"Intense." I bit my lip. "Scary."

"I'm sorry." He ran a hand through my hair, pushing the sweaty tendrils back from my forehead. "I didn't mean to scare you. Not for real."

I leaned up onto my elbows, still feeling off-kilter. "It wasn't scary like that, Kage. I trust you. I know you would never hurt me. It's just that… I came so *hard*. It's like I went somewhere else, but I was still coming."

I shuddered, unable to tell Kage the whole truth. That I felt like we'd crossed a line between reality and what ought to remain fantasy. And it was my fault.

(KAGE)

- 4:07 a.m. -

WHEN a fighter taps out in a choke, it's not something I want to miss. I'm waiting for it, every nerve ending on red alert, synapses waiting to give the signal to *let go, let go*!

But my muscles are tenacious, driven by an inborn need to conquer, to win, to survive. They lock on and won't let go, even through the little *tap-tap-tap* on my arm. And then even through the frantic slapping as he struggles to break free of my deadly grip, realizing too late the risk he's taken, that this is not a child's game. It's fucking Russian roulette, and he's lost. My embrace is going to drag him all the way down into death, and there's not a fucking thing he can do about it.

He lets loose in a flurry, slapping and tearing at my head, his compressed windpipe rasping out a last-ditch *"Kage, let me go!"*

Chapter

10

(JAMIE)

IN MY DREAM, Kage was behind me. He cradled my body within his, wrapping me up in the strangest, most wonderful sense of security I'd ever known. He was my lover and my keeper, my other half. We existed in our own little cocoon, hidden away from the rest of the world, floating untouched above the City of Sin.

But his hold on me, the one that kept me safe, tightened. His breathing became erratic against my ear, and his touch felt... different. The moment I woke up is the moment the dream turned into a nightmare.

Kage had wrapped himself around me like a hungry constrictor. I recognized the posture all too well.

My first reaction was panic, but then I thought maybe he was horsing around with me. I waited for a few seconds, hoping to feel his fevered nighttime kisses, or his erection sliding against my ass, but neither of those things happened. Instead, his strong arm went around my throat. I felt it like one of those automatic seat belts that cinch you up without permission.

My hands weren't quick enough or strong enough to stop him from executing the move. I cried out for him. "Let go, let go!" But he didn't let go. He squeezed harder. Not hard enough to damage my windpipe, but firmly enough to compromise the blood flow to my brain.

Then the full realization hit me of what was going on. Kage was killing me.

For a moment, time seemed to stand still. Right there in the middle of facing death, when my body should have been fleeing or fighting, my heart took the time to break.

Then my brain kicked into gear, and I started fighting for my life.

First I tried tapping out, but he didn't stop. I struggled against him with everything I had, realizing it just wasn't good enough. He was too damn strong, too single-minded, and too intent on killing me. I lashed out anyway, calling on every muscle in my body to not let this happen. My consciousness wavered, and the room got darker than dark. I tore at his hair, slapped at his head, clawed at his face. That's when I felt the wetness. Tears on his face. He was crying while he choked me.

I don't know why, but that one small detail made hope swell inside me, and I called on every ounce of vocal power I had left to call out to him. "Kage, let me go!"

Black spots still dominated my vision, and I was shaky as hell, but I was able to roll over and look at him where he'd collapsed onto the bed. Tears streamed from the corners of his eyes as he stared unseeing up at the ceiling, his chest heaving under a pale wash of moonlight. Something about him was not right, even aside from the fact that he'd just tried to kill me.

"Kage…" I whispered.

"Evan?" he whispered back.

My heart lodged in my throat. "Jamie," I said. "Kage, I'm Jamie."

He didn't say anything. He was so still and quiet, the tears trickling out of his eyes and running down his temples the only proof he was even alive. I shook him but he didn't move.

"Kage, are you okay? I know you were dreaming. Right?" He had been dreaming, hadn't he?

I couldn't get him to respond at all, and that scared me even worse than being choked to the threshold of death. I jumped from the bed, naked and frantic, running around his room to find his cell phone. I knew it was there, and yet somehow I couldn't get my brain to slow down long enough to focus on what I needed to do. "Phone," I said aloud to myself. "Gotta find the phone."

I finally located it on his bedside table and scrolled through his contacts, terrified that maybe in the phone switch he hadn't added Dr. Tanner's number to his contacts. But he had, and I called her, my hand shaking, my head telling me this could possibly be a huge mistake I was making. I didn't trust Dr. Tanner at all, and yet she was the only person I felt I could call. She was his therapist. She'd know what to do.

"Michael, what's wrong?" Her voice was alarmed, and that put me at ease. She wouldn't be alarmed if she didn't care, right?

"Dr. Tanner, this is Jamie."

"What is it, Jamie? Is Michael okay?"

"Not really. I need you at his place right now."

"I'm getting dressed right now, Jamie. It will take me twenty minutes to get there. Talk to me. Tell me what's happened."

"Well…" I glanced over at Kage, who was still catatonic on the bed. I wasn't sure how much I should tell her. I was afraid for him, and he couldn't tell me what he wanted me to do. "Kage was having a dream, I think. When I woke up, he was… uh… choking me."

"What?" Her alarm ratcheted even higher. "Do you mean like really choking you?"

I cleared my throat and looked at him again, wishing he'd wake up and tell me what to do. "He almost killed me."

I heard Dr. Tanner take a slow, deep breath. Then she did it again.

"What is he doing now? Is he still violent?"

"He's just lying still on the bed. Crying." The last word made *me* start crying. "He's just staring up at the ceiling. He won't talk to me. He called me Evan. That's all he said."

"His brother…" Dr. Tanner breathed.

"Yeah. I don't know what's going on, and I don't mind telling you I'm terrified. He almost killed me, Dr. Tanner. I was seconds away from going out, and if that had happened… he never would have let go."

"I'm driving now, Jamie. Try to stay calm. And whatever you do, stay away from him. I don't know if he'll try it again. Keep an eye on him, but keep your distance, too. Can you do that for me?"

"Yes. Please hurry, Dr. Tanner."

She stayed on the phone during the drive, just in case anything happened. Most of the time we just sat in silence while she drove and I watched over Kage. He finally moved a little, but only enough to curl onto his side. The tears had stopped, and I wondered if it was because he didn't have any left.

When Dr. Tanner knocked on the door, I ran to let her in.

"You look like hell," she said.

"I think I just almost went there."

She moved to Kage's bedside and pulled out her medical bag. Then she began to inspect him.

"I, uh… You said don't touch him, so he's not wearing anything."

"I can see that," she said. "Come over here and get something on him." I did as she instructed, and after his modesty was protected by a pair of boxer briefs she resumed. "Michael, can you hear me? How are you feeling?"

He didn't respond.

"I'm going to medicate him." She pulled out a syringe and injected something into his arm.

"What are you giving him?"

"Lorazepam. It will help him snap out of this catatonic state he's in."

"What the fuck is wrong with him, Dr. Tanner. And be straight with me. No more lies."

She sighed, capped the syringe, and disposed of it in the wastebasket. "Alright, Jamie. I'm going to tell you what I know, but you have to promise to keep quiet. Michael has already told me he trusts you, and that he wants you to be a part of his life. I advised him to keep certain things from you, because I wanted to protect him. He's a prime candidate for extortion, if you hadn't noticed. But I suppose by now you've proven your loyalty. If you're willing to stand by him after he's nearly killed you... well, that says something."

"Tell, me," I prompted, weary of the banter.

"I haven't worked with him the entire time since his uncle adopted him, you understand. I'm not the first therapist he had. By the time I came along, he had buried his memories of his family so far down, I don't even think he knows he has them. I suspect the therapy he received as a young child was geared toward helping him repress those memories. At the very least, they did nothing to help retrieve them. But there was some sort of childhood trauma. I know this, because Michael suffers from PTSD. That's what these episodes you have witnessed are."

"Something to do with his brother?"

"Yes." She bit her lip, considering how much she should tell me.

"Just say it," I told her. "At this point, what is it going to hurt?"

She sat down on the side of the bed. I glanced over at Kage, wondering why it was that every time I had to call his therapist to come over, he had to be dressed inappropriately or not at all. It made me sad for him, underscoring his helplessness. But I wasn't about to touch him and get dragged back into a choke. I had no doubt that he could finish the job, even with Dr. Tanner in the room. He could kill either or both of us if he wanted.

"Michael's brother Evan was older than him, though only by a year. When Michael was five and Evan was six, they discovered their mother dead of an overdose. A couple of years later, their father was in such bad shape he brought them here to get help from Mr. Santori. Evan died soon after. I was told the boys were playing, and that there was an accident— a fall or something. Michael felt responsible, since he was present and had to witness it. That must have been so horrible for him, and so soon after finding his mother's body. Michael says he can't remember what happened to his brother, and his uncle has ordered me in no uncertain terms to let it be. He doesn't want Michael to remember, because it would be too traumatic for him to have to relive it."

"Do you agree with that?" I asked, sensing that she didn't.

"Absolutely not. I see what these repressed memories are doing to him. You see it, too. How can he ever move past it if he can't call up the memories and deal with them? As his therapist, my hands are tied. It's impossible to treat him for something I can't see. I just have no idea what we're up against, and everyone else is content to keep it that way."

"You couldn't just do it on your own? Hypnotize him or something?"

She snorted. "Santori said he would fire me. And worse. He practically supports me, you know. The kind of money he pays me, I couldn't get anywhere else." She turned and stared down at Kage's motionless form. "But seeing him like this makes me wonder if it's worth it."

"He's really a nice person. Everybody acts like he's something... I don't know. *Hard*. But he's not really. Not to me."

"He cares about you." Dr. Tanner glanced away from me and dabbed at the corners of her eyes with her fingertips. "Which is a miracle in itself. That boy has been so alone in his life. Even surrounded by people, he just never made the connections. He's good at blending, though. He can do as the natives do, so to speak, but he's not really there. Part of him is still that seven-year-old boy who was never able to move on from the trauma of losing his whole family in the span of two years. The other part of him is boarded up and hidden from the world. How you ever got inside is beyond me."

"You're inside, too," I said. "You know him."

"Not as well as I should. Because of selfish reasons, I've let things go that I should have done something about. I should never have let Santori talk me into coming to see you that day, before you left to go back to school. I didn't want to do it. I knew how he felt about you, and I did it anyway."

I walked over to the window and stared out, feeling a twinge in my belly at the sight of the clear balcony where Kage had made me come so hard. Where he'd asked me if I would risk my life for him. Now he'd forced me to prove it, and I wasn't sure how I felt about that.

He was mine, and I loved him. But fuck if the man wasn't dangerous.

11

(JAMIE)

Hours later, after the sun had come up and exposed us all in our misery, Kage started talking. He started talking, and what he said changed all of our lives forever.

"Mommy," he mumbled, and Dr. Tanner and I both started.

"Yes, baby," she said, moving to his side and taking his hand.

I grimaced, wondering what the hell she thought she was doing, and at the same time thinking it might just work to get some information out of him. Coercion of a catatonic guy in the throes of a PTSD attack seemed sketchy at best, but Dr. Tanner had said she couldn't treat him without knowing what she was up against. At this point, I was all for anything that would help Kage deal with whatever it was that was destroying him inside. And now that my life had been threatened, it seemed even more important to get at the truth. Otherwise, I'd be dead, and Kage would be in prison.

Kage didn't fall for the bait and switch, though. "Dr. Tanner, I fucked up." His words were slurry and slow coming out.

"What did you do, Michael?"

"Nothing."

"If you tell me, I can help you."

"I didn't do anything."

"Maybe if you'd tell me—"

"I didn't do it!" he screamed. Then his voice was quiet. "I didn't do it."

"Of course you didn't," she said calmly.

I stalked away from the bed, fighting the anxiety that coiled up in my chest and made the back of my neck tingle.

Dr. Tanner continued to talk to him in a controlled voice. "I need you to stay calm for me, Michael. Everything is going to be okay. Isn't everything always okay after we talk?"

He nodded, and I could see his tight swallow from where I was standing near the window. He was on his back again, and Dr. Tanner had propped him up with an extra pillow under his shoulders. His body looked relaxed, but his throat kept pulsing with those hard swallows, and his eyebrows were drawn inward.

"I know how to make everything okay, right?" Dr. Tanner asked.

"Right," Kage said.

"That's why you call me when you're in trouble."

He nodded again.

"I want you to do something for me," she said. "A relaxation exercise. I want you to keep your eyes closed and take a deep breath. Then let it out at your own slow pace."

He did as she instructed, and she led him through a series of five more breaths. By the time she was finished, his brows had relaxed, and he was swallowing normally.

She continued in that gentle, even voice. "I want you to picture yourself, Michael. You're seven years old now. Just picture yourself as that seven-year-old boy, standing outside the Alcazar with your family on the first day you arrived in Las Vegas."

"I can't picture my mom there," he said. "She's dead. She never got to see Vegas."

"Yes, I'm sorry to hear that. Can you picture your dad and your brother Evan?"

"Yes. They can be there."

"Good. Now, I don't want you to feel, Michael. There's no need for you to feel right now. You only need to see and report. Can you do that?"

"You don't want me to feel? You always encourage me to feel, even if it's bad."

"I know that. But today, I don't want you to feel. I'm letting you off the hook, because I've someone here who can do the feeling for you." She spared a glance at me. "So just seeing and reporting, not feeling, tell me what you see. Are you standing outside the Alcazar?"

"Yes. It's big."

"And who is with you?"

His head moved almost imperceptibly from side to side, as if in his mind he was really looking. "My dad and Evan. God, I'd forgotten how dirty they were. How their clothes were old. How my dad wore a plaid shirt under that Army jacket, and his corduroy pants smelled like cigarettes when I leaned against his leg. How Evan's hair was greasy and stuck up in places," he laughed, and it dissolved into something like a whimper.

Dr. Tanner quickly stepped in. "What does the building look like, Michael? Do you see your uncle?"

"Santori," he said. "That's not my dad's name. Not my name."

"What is your name?" she prompted.

"I don't know. But that's what my dad said. Our name is not Santori. My uncle is Santori. *Mister Santori to you. Get your urchins upstairs to the bath before someone calls social services.*"

He seemed to be spouting off random quotes from his memory, all in his own voice, and I marveled at how strong that memory must be in his head to allow him to just fall right into it like that. I could hardly remember anything I'd said last week, and here Kage was reciting stuff from seventeen years before.

"Do you like Mr. Santori?" Dr. Tanner asked.

"He's got ice cream," he said. "*There's pistachio ice cream in the kitchen, and if you're a good boy and do what I say, you can have some. We don't get ice cream very often, and pistachio is my favorite. I hope it comes on a cone.*"

It was eerie how Kage kept saying Santori's lines.

"Did you get the ice cream?" Dr. Tanner asked.

"Not yet. I ask him sometimes, but he keeps forgetting. He's a busy man with a hotel to run."

"What does your father do at the hotel?"

"He keeps losing his ass. They're gonna cut him off. He wouldn't know luck if it hit him upside the head. He doesn't have the Santori blood. If he had the Santori blood, he could win."

I hung my head, hurting inside for the little kid who had to hear all of that nonsense. Santori could crush the soul of a grown man. I couldn't even imagine how intimidating he must have been to a seven-year-old boy.

"Let's remember to not feel, Michael," Dr. Tanner said. "We're only seeing and reporting. It's not necessary to feel."

Kage nodded, still keeping his eyes closed. I had to hand it to the therapist. She was doing a good job of keeping him calm, even when he was exploring painful memories that he may have kept buried for years.

"Do you remember playing with Evan at the Alcazar?" Dr. Tanner tried to keep her voice steady, but I could hear the slight change in it. I worried that Kage would notice and shut down on us.

"Yeah, I remember. We had fun. We could run up and down the halls as long as we didn't get caught. We could play in the stairwells.

My dad won at cards one time, and he bought us these big plastic dump trucks. There wasn't any sand, but we would let them go down the stairs." He laughed, and Dr. Tanner reminded him again about not feeling.

I wished she could make me not feel, because as Kage described the way he and his brother used to play on the stairs, my stomach began to knot up to the point of pain. To have a forgotten story of tragedy unfolding right before me terrified me in a way that nearly surpassed having the life choked out of me. If things got much more intense, and I had a feeling they would, I was afraid I might throw up.

"Did anything happen on the stairs, Michael?"

I sucked in a sharp breath at her bold question, and she shot me a glare— a wordless admonition to shut the hell up before I ruined everything.

"My truck broke," Kage said. "Evan threw his down and broke it, too, so we would both have broken trucks. There wasn't any sand, anyway."

Tears welled up in my eyes. God, why did we have to listen to this? Why did this have to be Kage's life? I was already freaking out, and we hadn't even gotten to the part where his brother died. Jesus Christ, I did not want to hear that. But I had no choice. Kage was mine now, and this was part of what shaped him and haunted him. If I wanted him— and I did, so much— then I would have to take all of this, too. I'd known almost from the start that he needed someone to help shoulder his burden, and I also knew I was the one he'd chosen for the job. But in my inexperience, I hadn't been capable of imagining how real that burden might be. Now I was getting a crash course.

On the bed, Kage smiled at nothing, still keeping his eyes closed. It was comforting to know that inside his head, he was getting to relive a little of the joy he'd experienced before his brother died.

"No feelings this time, Michael," Dr. Tanner reminded. "We can do that another time. Right now, we're only seeing."

The smile faded from Kage's face.

Dr. Tanner took a deep, steadying breath before proceeding. "Do you remember the last time you saw Evan?"

Kage didn't answer at first. His face was stone, and he'd gone so still he couldn't have been breathing.

"They wanted us to do it. We didn't want to. Evan didn't like it when they made us fight."

My skin broke out in cold gooseflesh, and all the blood drained from my face. Dr. Tanner went rigid.

"Who wanted you to do it?" she asked carefully.

"Mister Santori and the other men. They liked to drink beer at Mr. Santori's place, and they wanted to bet on us. They'd done it once before, and Evan won. Then he cried, because he said he didn't like hitting me for real. I told him it was okay, that it didn't really hurt all that much. My dad didn't like it, either. It was after our bedtime— we had real beds then— and we needed to rest up. But Mr. Santori said we had to do it. His friends wanted to bet, and if my dad wanted us to stay, we were going to have to fight."

"Are you saying they bet on you and your brother to fight? To see who would win?"

Kage nodded. "He made my dad bet, and my dad picked Evan. Mr. Santori picked me."

"And who won, Michael?" Dr. Tanner leaned in toward him, her face ashen.

"I don't know." Kage said. "I don't want to fight. Don't make me fight."

"Who won?"

"He wouldn't hit me, and he wouldn't kick me. He just sat down on the floor. I didn't want to fight him, but Santori made me. I got him in a rear naked choke, and he was supposed to tap out like we always did. But he wouldn't tap. Santori kept telling him to tap out, but he wouldn't. I tried to let go."

His voice was laced with fear, and I couldn't stand for him to go through any more pain. It was killing me. Tears were streaming down my face, and I grabbed Dr. Tanner's shoulder and said, "That's enough."

Dr. Tanner backhanded me across the face. I felt the sting of her diamond wedding ring as it sliced through my lip. Then she glanced sheepishly up at me, and unspoken apology in her eyes. The slap had gotten my attention, though, reminding me that this was the first breakthrough Kage had ever had, and if his therapist was going to help him, she needed to get the whole story.

I took a step back and steeled myself.

Kage was crying again, and I suspected that telling him not to feel wouldn't have the same effect on him anymore. Dr. Tanner didn't even try. She just asked, "What happened then?"

"I said I was going to let go. Evan wouldn't tap out, and it felt like he went limp, but I wasn't sure. Everyone was yelling at me. And my dad was yelling at Evan to tap out. He tried to get over to us, but Santori grabbed him by the arm and held him back. Santori yelled, 'Don't let go until he taps out." I told him I was going to let go, but he said, 'You let go, and you won't get any pistachio ice cream.'" Kage whimpered, and his face contorted with emotion. "I wanted my ice cream, so I held on tight. Evan didn't tap out, and he didn't move anymore. I just wanted my ice cream, that's all."

Kage broke down then. Neither Dr. Tanner nor I could understand much of what he said after that. Just a word here and there. "I just wanted my ice cream cone," he mumbled once, a child's plea for understanding. For forgiveness. Hearing him like that demolished me. My shoulders shook with the effort to keep him from hearing me cry.

Dr. Tanner stepped out onto the balcony to collect herself, and I could hear her choked sobs through the glass. When she finally returned, red-eyed and taking deep, slow breaths, she took mercy on the whimpering wreck that was my boyfriend. She started talking him back up out of the trance-like state she'd induced.

"You will remember everything we've talked about," she said, and I cringed. I wasn't so sure Kage ought to remember that shit. I know I wanted to forget it.

DR. TANNER KEPT Kage doped up for the rest of the day. I was supposed to fly back home the day after that, but I didn't want to go.

She and I stood over him as he slept on the bed, and we argued about whether or not I was going to get on that plane.

"He needs me," I said.

The therapist looked at me with hollowed out eyes. "You can't do anything for him right now. I just need to ease him back around to a good frame of mind, okay? He needs therapy, and I need to taper off these meds I've been giving him. You can't say anything to a soul about what has gone on here this weekend, Jamie. You understand that, right? This is sensitive information, and it's Kage's business."

I was too tired and wrung out from worry to be offended at the implication that I would go around blabbing about Kage's personal life. "Of course I would never say anything. I care about him. I love him." I ran a hand over my face and debated with myself over whether or not to bring up the elephant in the room. But it had to be addressed if Kage and I were going to be together. "What about the choking thing? You and I haven't really discussed it, and I was wondering if it was, you know... safe for me."

"I don't know," she said. "Honestly, I don't. I'll need to assess him when he's not medicated like this. My initial feeling is that this was a one-time incident. Now that his memory is no longer repressed and his conscious mind can finally deal with it, his subconscious can stop fighting so hard to make him remember. Do you have any idea what could have been the trigger for this? There's usually something significant that happens to cause it to surge up."

"Um..." I toed the floor, turned away and paced to the balcony. "I think I do know what the trigger was, but I'm embarrassed to tell you."

"Why would you be embarrassed?"

172

I laughed and ran a hand nervously through my hair. "Oh, there are several reasons. Number one: it was my fault, number two: it was sexual, and number three: it was really fucked up."

Dr. Tanner rolled her eyes to the ceiling and crossed her arms like an angry mother. "What was it? Spit it out."

"Well, there were these comments online, and one of them was a guy saying he'd love to have Kage choke him out. But in a sexual way."

"Jamie, do you know how dangerous that is?"

I snorted humorlessly. "I do now. At the time, I was just thinking he'd like it. Because, you know..." I glanced up at her, waiting for her to give some indication that she knew where I was going with this.

"I know what?" she prompted.

"That he likes his sex a little on the hardcore side."

"As a matter of fact, I know many things about him, and that is one of them. But you say *he* likes it on the hardcore side. Does that mean you don't?"

"Well, I..." My face started to get hot. "I never did anything like that before. Then I met him, and he was so persuasive."

"So he coerced you into doing things you didn't want to do?"

"No! God, why do I feel like you're trying to psychoanalyze me?" Kage stirred on the bed in response to my outburst, and I dropped my voice. I didn't want to disturb his rest, and I also didn't exactly want him to hear me talking about our sex life and all of the weird feelings that might go along with it. "All right, Dr. Tanner. Yes, I do like it. I like it very much. It's just that, before I met Kage, I had no idea I had urges like that. In fact, he's the first guy I've ever been with. I'd always been with girls before. Does that satisfy your curiosity?"

"Actually, it's not curiosity. You happen to be dating my patient, and he can't speak for himself right now. His sex life is directly related to the situation, since your activities apparently triggered a PTSD episode, and you are exactly one half of that sex life. So I think my questions are reasonable, don't you?"

"Fine. I get it. It's just embarrassing to have to admit some of these things."

"I know about what happened at your parents' house, Jamie."

My eyes went wide. "The pantry? When did he tell you about that? It just happened a couple of weeks ago."

"I'm referring to the incident in the yard," she said. "He said he'd hurt you. How do you feel about that?"

I shrugged. "I couldn't wait to see him again. If you're thinking he did something I didn't want that night, you're wrong. I love everything he does to me."

She took a deep breath and studied Kage's sleeping form. His chest rose and fell rhythmically, and his face was relaxed. He was at peace for the time being, and that loosened the tightness in my chest and made me feel hopeful again. "I'd like for you guys to be more careful from now on, okay? Less impulsive, at least for a while until we know that he's getting better. We don't want any more surprises like last night."

"But you said you thought it was because his memories were repressed, and now they're not repressed anymore. Right?"

"That's right. And in my experience, that is an accurate assessment. I'm just asking you to be cautious for a while."

I nodded. "Okay. We'll be cautious."

"In the meantime, you will go back to school and focus on your studies. That's what he would want you to do, and you know it. He would feel guilty if he found out you had flunked out of school because of his episode, and the last thing he needs is more guilt."

The discussion about school brought back memories of the previous discussion I'd had with Dr. Tanner about the same subject. "Last time you told me to go back to school, you were helping Santori get rid of me. How do I know I can trust you now?"

Her face went hard, and she shot a menacing look toward Santori's apartment. "That bastard is the last person I would ever help. After what we learned here yesterday, do you actually think I would have any loyalty left? I would kill him dead if I thought I could get away with it. As it is, I'm going to confront him and see what he has to say for himself. His reign of terror over Michael is over as far as I'm concerned."

"You're really going to confront him?" I asked. "That's either really brave or really stupid."

She laughed. "A little of both, I'm sure. But don't you worry. You go back to school and do your thing. I want to watch Michael for a couple of weeks before you see him again. I think it's important for me to help him work through all of this first. But I promise, this is only going to be good for the two of you. As soon as I think he's settled enough to see you, he'll order a plane ticket and fly you back out for the weekend."

"A couple of weeks?"

"A couple of weeks. Three at the most."

I left reluctantly, but I knew Dr. Tanner was right. Kage needed her more than he needed me right now. And as soon as he was ready, I would be on a plane to see him. Then we could put into effect his two day plan and live happily ever after.

12

(KAGE)

I SLAMMED THE phone down on the bed, resisting the urge to follow up with a fist through the wall. A quick phone call to the airport had just confirmed what I'd already suspected. No delays. The fucking plane had made it on time, and still no Jamie.

Dr. Tanner and I had been talking for three weeks, and she'd helped me come to terms with the death of my brother. It was strange, but the memory of how my brother died had brought with it a certain peace I hadn't had before. Dr. Tanner felt like it was because I'd known the truth all along, but my mind just hadn't wanted to admit it.

We hadn't had a therapy session in days, but I felt strong on my own now. She still didn't think I should see Santori if I could help it, and I had to agree with her on that. As much as I felt I had made progress, I still wasn't ready to face him. I was, however, ready to see Jamie. More than ready, in fact. He'd called every day to check on me, and after a week Dr. Tanner had let me start talking to him again. Now he was supposed to be coming to visit, and I should have been overjoyed, not wondering where the hell he was.

I paced to the balcony and stepped outside, dragging in a deep breath and staring out over the city I called home. The view did nothing to settle my nerves, because I knew better than most what darkness lurked beneath the jaunty veneer. My uncle had built an empire on it.

Jamie was not safe. I knew it in my gut, yet I'd gone ahead with the plan to bring him out for the weekend. The rationalization that he'd be just as safe here as anywhere felt faulty now, and I was kicking myself. He and I could be holed up in his bedroom in Georgia right now, working out a plan to extract ourselves from my uncle's web of crazy. I was convinced more than ever that throwing myself a big coming out party and inviting the media was the best course of action, because without the secret of my sexuality to protect, my uncle had no motivation to do anything bad to Jamie.

Well, none except meanness, and I wasn't naïve enough to discount that at all.

I went back into the room and picked up my phone, trying to figure out who I could call to find out if Jamie had even gotten on the plane. Braden would probably know. I scrolled through what few contacts I had programmed in and selected Braden's name, hoping he'd even recognize my number and pick up.

"Hello?" he asked tentatively on the third ring.

"Braden, so glad I got you. Did Jamie get on the plane today? He was supposed to come visit me."

"Kage?" His voice was excited.

"Yeah, man. I don't have time to talk. I'm worried about Jamie. Did he get on the plane?"

"I think so. He said he was going to Vegas. His SUV is gone, so I'm assuming he left it in airport parking."

"Okay, thanks."

Braden assured me that he'd let me know if he heard anything before we ended the call. I had a really bad feeling. There was no legitimate reason for Jamie to be late and not answering calls or texts, especially when the flight had been on time.

I was just about to try Dr. Tanner again when my phone rang. Jamie's name popped up on the screen, and relief flooded my system. Thank God he was okay.

"Hey, baby," I said in greeting, hating that I sounded so needy.

"Hey," he said back, not sounding needy at all. "Um, I guess you're wondering why I'm not there."

"A little. Where are you?"

"Well, actually I'm still in Georgia. I never got on the plane."

Part of me felt relieved. Now I could just go to him there. Far away from my uncle and his bullshit.

"I've been doing a lot of thinking," he continued. "Things have been getting a little crazy lately with your uncle, and people spying on us. And now with you having the episode. It's just too much, Kage. You need to focus on your health and your career, and I need to finish school. I haven't been able to pay attention in class for worrying about all this stuff."

"I can make all of the bad stuff go away. I'm working on it right now, Jamie. I have a plan."

"I don't know. I think it's too late to go back. Now that I've made up my mind, it seems like the best thing for me would be to find someone who fits better with my lifestyle, you know?"

"Cameron," I growled. "Is that it? Eddie Haskell wasn't good enough for you, and now you want to get some real country club action? If you think that's going to satisfy you, you're in for a rude awakening."

"Kage… That's ridiculous."

"Is it?"

The silence on the other end of the line sounded like confirmation that he was moving on. Hell, there wasn't even any emotion in his voice. How could he sound so calm when I was losing my shit? How could he not feel something?

"I'll figure out some way to get the Rover back to you," he said.

"Keep it."

"I can't do that. It costs too much."

I channeled all the anger I was feeling into my words. "I don't want anything from you. It's paid for. Sell it and use the money as a down payment on that dream house you were talking about. Maybe you and Cameron can get a place right on the golf course. Something with a cute little picket fence."

"I swear to you this has nothing to do with Cameron. I just can't take the stress anymore. You don't get what it's like for me, because you've lived in it your entire life. Hell, I don't know anything but sports, college classes, and family dinners. The biggest drama I ever had was trying to pass my finals without studying. But now…" His voice dropped low, and his words were deliberate. "There are life and death stakes involved here, Kage. Do you hear what I'm saying? I still love you. I'll always love you. But I have to go, okay?"

"I'm sorry." Damn my voice for sounding so weak. "I'm sorry for the drama. I can do better. I'll be stronger and stand up for myself. I'm going to tell them, Jamie. Monday morning, I'll contact the biggest sports blogs and give a statement, and then it will all be over. We can go somewhere else and build a life together, even if the UFC doesn't want me anymore. You'll have your degree, and I can coach or something. We could start a gym."

I was pleading, and I didn't care, because Jamie was just going to walk away. How much more could I lose and still want to go on? I fucking hated feeling sorry for myself, but dammit, I needed *something* to live for. Something besides fighting.

There was a weighted pause on the other end of the line. My breathing sped up. Then Jamie cleared his throat.

"All of that sounds great, Kage. But it's just too late. My mind is made up. I think this will be better for both of us."

"So you're just gonna end it like that? It's that easy for you?"

"Yes."

"Alright, Jamie." I tightened my grip on the phone and moved to look out the window again, not really seeing this time. "But I want you to understand one thing. There's going to come a time when you want to come back. I know you, and I know you can't stay away. If you wake up tomorrow and realize you've made a mistake and want to come back, I'll be here for you. You can tell me you were wrong, and we'll kiss and make up, and everything will be back to the way it was." I swallowed and turned my back to the window, shifting the phone to the other ear. "But the minute you fuck someone else, that option is gone. There's no coming back from that. I'll still want you, but I'll never touch you again. And all of the things I do to you, the things that turn you inside out, I'll be doing to someone else. You'd better make damn sure you can live with that."

I clicked off, not wanting to hear any more of his empty apologies and excuses. The bottom line was he didn't want me. For whatever reasons, and for however long, he didn't want me. And it fucking hurt.

I did the only thing I could think of. I called Dr. Tanner. She would know what to say to make me feel better, or at the very least come over with some good pharmaceuticals to make everything okay for a little while. But she didn't answer her cell again. It was the third time I'd called in two days, and she still hadn't returned my calls. That wasn't like her. Maybe she'd had enough of my drama, too. It was bad when even my psychiatrist couldn't handle the crazy.

But I needed her. I was still raw from the hypnosis session and the disturbing memories that had surfaced as a result, and now Jamie had left me. If there was ever a time I needed some therapy, or just a shoulder to cry on, it was now.

I'd always had Dr. Tanner's cell number, so there was no reason for me to know her office number. I went online and looked it up. Maybe my uncle had managed to get her cell phone blocked, too.

Dr. Tanner's office phone rang twice before a man picked up. "Hello?" he said, which I thought was an odd greeting for a business office.

"Uh, is this Dr. Tanner's office?"

"It is."

"My name is Michael Santori. I'm a patient of Dr. Tanner's. I've been trying to call her cell, but she hasn't answered. I thought maybe her phone service is out or something?"

"This is Kage?" the man asked, suddenly sounding more alert. "This is Julie's— uh, Dr. Tanner's— husband, Dale. I don't know how to tell you this other than to come right out with it. Julie has been missing for two days."

"What?" The room swam. "Are you sure? There's nowhere she could be?" I sounded like an idiot, but I couldn't process the information properly. And my mind had already suggested something so horrific I felt guilty for even thinking it.

Dr. Tanner had disappeared right around the last time I'd seen her. Oh, God. What if she'd confronted my uncle after she left my apartment? What if she'd told him what she'd discovered, and that she knew what he'd done? What if her disappearance was all my fault?

And then on the heels of that thought came one that was even worse. One that stopped me dead in my tracks as I paced the room.

Both Jamie and Dr. Tanner witnessed my hypnosis. As far as I knew, they were the only two people besides my uncle who knew the truth about my past. Could it possibly be a coincidence that they had both disappeared from my life in a matter of a few days? Somehow I didn't think so.

"I'm sorry to hear Dr. Tanner is missing," I said, suddenly remembering Mr. Tanner was on the phone. "I know you must be worried sick. Please let me know if I can do anything to help you find her."

"Thank you, Kage. I'll keep you posted."

I could not get off of the phone fast enough. If my suspicions were true, and Jamie was in danger, I had to take action immediately. Before, I hadn't actually thought my uncle capable of harming Jamie in a physical way. Maybe I just hadn't wanted to believe it, because there was certainly enough evidence to the contrary. But now that Dr. Tanner had gone missing— and let's face it, *gone missing* usually meant they just hadn't found the body yet— I was in a dead panic.

I obsessed over Jamie's phone call, trying to remember every word. *Jesus Christ, what had he said?* I'd been such a mess about him breaking up with me, I hadn't thought to listen for clues. How could I have known? *God, I should have known.*

At the very least, I was certain my uncle had coerced him into making the call, and clearly Jamie had cooperated. That was a good sign, wasn't it? But I felt guilty about the petty comments I'd made about Cameron, and about Jamie being with other people. Because right now I was thinking I'd rather watch him bang the entire student body of Georgia State University than to know that one hair on his head was in danger.

13

(JAMIE)

IN RETROSPECT, I probably should have run when I saw that Aldo and Aaron had been dispatched to retrieve me from the Vegas airport. It was pretty stupid to climb into the back of a limo driven by the very people I suspected of spying on me. But then nothing had made much sense in my life since I'd met Michael Kage. It felt like I was in a perpetual dream that morphed into a nightmare every few days. There were no rules.

I had definitely been watched, and calls had been intercepted and blocked. But those were the only concrete things we knew. The threat of danger had only been a vague hint, and nothing had been done to make it seem imminent. It hadn't occurred to me that, if a smart guy like Santori wanted to do something bad to me, he would make sure I didn't see it coming. The problem is that I'd underestimated him. Intellectually, I'd known he was smart and powerful. Instinctively, I'd known he was capable of evil without remorse. Now I knew what he'd done to Kage seventeen years before. The coming together of those three things in my mind should have made a din to rival the bells of Christ Church Cathedral. Only it didn't. Somehow I'd just let the knowledge sit there like little innocuous puzzle pieces, not even worth my consideration. I had more important things to worry about, like sex, and jealousy, and whether or not Kage should spend money on me.

As I sat there in the back of the Range Rover limo, listening to Aldo report to someone on the other end of a phone call— *"I've picked up the package. What do you want me to do with it?"*— it occurred to me that maybe I should have fucking listened all those times Kage called me clueless. Because I was. God help me, I was a fucking idiot, and now something bad was going to happen to me. I just knew it, especially when Aldo ordered me to surrender my phone to Aaron.

By the time we arrived at the warehouse where I'd seen Kage fight for the first time, I was trembling like I had a fever. My teeth were chattering. All I could think of was how I'd seen this coming. The last time Aldo and Aaron had driven me out to the very same spot, I'd had terrible fantasies of being murdered mafia style and dumped in the desert. The irony of it would have made me laugh, if I hadn't been about to throw up.

As we entered the building, the heavy door screamed on its hinges, and dust particles swam within the swath of light that cut through the darkness. It was tomb quiet inside. No glitterati, no excitement. Just a dank odor, stacks of chairs, and the forsaken octagon looming in the shadows.

Aldo grabbed a couple of chairs and shoved me down into one.

"Where's Kage?" I finally managed to ask.

"He's at his apartment waiting for you," Aldo said. "But here's the thing. You're not going there."

"Where am I going?" I squeaked.

"Well, that depends on you. Whether you decide to be smart for once, or be a little shit disturber like usual."

"Smart sounds good," I admitted without thinking. Because it did. Being smart sounded really freaking good right now.

"Maybe this is gonna be easier than I thought." Aldo glanced over at Aaron, who was running a hand absently over his buzzed head while he perused my phone. The two of them looked so much alike, with their caps of stubble and nondescript faces. It was no wonder my property manager was unable to give a good description of the man who had complained about my blinds being open. I imagined guys like these could easily slip in and out of a crime scene leaving witnesses with only a vague impression of what they'd looked like. Just a couple of guys in suits. For a hired goon, being unremarkable probably looked good on a resumé. I filed that bit of information away, just in case I made it out in one piece and wanted to turn to a life of crime.

But I still wasn't sure which one of them had complained. Knowing that would have helped, considering the complaint had felt like a friendly warning. If one of these guys was a friend, I sure as hell needed to know which one.

"Here's the deal, *Jamie.*" Aldo overenunciated my name, as if he found it— or me— distasteful. "Mr. Santori doesn't like you. Actually, I'm sure it will come as no surprise to you that he hates your fucking faggoty little guts."

"Ooh, colorful insult. Did you come up with that all on your own, or did Santori tell you what to say?" The sarcasm spilled out of me, confirming that I had in fact not suddenly become smart. I was about to be killed, and here I was taunting my would-be murderer without so much as a stutter. Definitely not smart. But Aldo surprised me. Instead of backhanding me across the jaw or putting a bullet in my forehead, he just smiled.

"I ad lib sometimes. Keeps the job fresh." He pushed a chair in front of me and indicated that I should sit down. "The sentiment is all Santori's, though. He's the one pulling the strings, and he's the one who says who gets to live or die."

I swallowed and sat down, glancing over at Aaron for... anything. But he was just fiddling with my phone, probably looking at the naked selfies I'd sent Kage. Like the stalker hadn't seen enough of my ass. Jesus, why did that man even exist? I'd never seen him actually do anything. He didn't drive, he didn't speak. If he'd done any less, he'd have been dead.

"So, do I get to live or die?" I asked, wondering if my stupidity had bounds, or if it could keep increasing indefinitely.

"Live." Aldo said without hesitation, and all of the breath came out of me in one long sigh of relief. "Kage is the one who's going to die."

And suddenly I was floating, in danger of losing consciousness, because of all of the things I could have imagined them threatening,

Kage's life was not one of them. It shocked me to discover in such a tangible way that I actually placed more value on Kage's life than I did my own. The fear that settled over me at Aldo's words was mentally debilitating. All sarcasm had left the building.

"Why?" I breathed, fearing the answer.

"Because of you. His uncle can't control him anymore, and just between you and me, Santori's got no use for somebody he can't control. He's been training that boy practically since he was in diapers, and now he just won't cooperate with the plan. Not since you came along." Aldo shook his head as he regarded me. "I don't know what it is about you that he thinks is so damn special. He could have anybody. That model is in love with him, always has been, but you know that. It ain't no secret. But Kage has always been about the D, you know? Always chasing the dick. We've seen a lot." He chuckled and shot a meaningful glance in Aaron's direction, but the other goon declined to react. "If you'd seen the shit we've seen, the messes we've had to clean up…"

"What are you telling me?" I swallowed back a flood of bile and tried to shut out the grainy pictures that were threatening to become clear in my mind.

"You might not know this, but anonymous sex ain't always anonymous. Not when you're as recognizable as Michael Kage Santori. He never could understand the risks, or maybe he just didn't care, I don't know. Whatever the reasons, he never could keep it in his pants, you know? Refused to play by the rules. Every time he fought, we'd have to be on standby. Fun times down at the Tick-Tock, right Aaron? With Mr. John Brown." He raised his brows at his companion and smiled. "Had to watch that shit. Keep an eye on things, because it could get ugly in the blink of an eye. Remember that one kid with the piercing? Little emo fucker. He was the first one that went south." He looked at me and continued, as if he was just telling a funny story from his college days. "This kid had metal everywhere. Had a goddamn metal hook through the head of his dick." He shook his head and winced. "Anyway, this stupid fucker had a thing for getting knocked around, right? And our boy Kage, well, you know how good he is at that kind of thing. So the two of them hook up, but the thing is, this boy recognizes him. Or maybe he already knew who he was before he set up the date. You see where I'm going with this?"

I wasn't sure that I did. All I could picture was Kage's talented tongue dancing around a big fat Prince Albert piercing. Even under the threat of death, I was jealous. He'd done that to me.

"Um… he told somebody, and Kage almost got outed?"

Aldo laughed. "Not quite. Next day we get a call that this kid has shown up at the hotel, demanding to see Santori, and he's got fucking bruises all over him. Looks like hell. Says your boyfriend raped him and beat the shit out of him, and he's got DNA proof. See these so-called rape victims can go down to the hospital and get a rape kit done for free, but they don't have to press charges. Not right then. They seal all that DNA evidence up, along with the details about the injuries, and then the police come down and get it. Then the victim has a year or so to decide if they want to report the assault."

I thought of the night Kage first came to my parents' house. How Layla had tried to get me to go to the hospital and do a rape kit.

My stomach churned, and I closed my eyes, listening to Aldo blather on.

"Imagine how mad Santori got when he found out his kid's DNA is just sitting down at the precinct. That he's that close to being ruined. Of course it was all about money. The guy demanded some outrageous amount of money to keep from pressing charges. Said the DNA evidence was his insurance policy, like he was some big shot who knew what he was doing."

Aldo shook his head and laughed. I waited for the end of the story, but he didn't offer it. Instead, he pulled out his phone and checked it, remarking to Aaron that he'd received the text message he'd been expecting.

"Kage never went to jail," I pointed out. "Did Santori pay the guy off?"

"Nope." Aldo pulled up a chair and sat down facing me, our knees nearly touching. "The DNA evidence disappeared. Somebody fucked up with the filing or something."

"And the emo kid?"

"He disappeared, too." Aldo cracked his knuckles and leaned toward me. He didn't have to tell me he'd been the one to make the kid disappear. I may have been an idiot, but I'd taken enough English classes to recognize the moral of this story.

"So I don't understand why you said Kage was in danger. Why would his uncle go to such great lengths to protect him if he's just going to turn around and hurt him?"

"A man can only invest in a loser for just so long before he's either got to cut his losses and get out, or become a loser himself."

"Has he tried talking to Kage? Reasoning with him? Kage is a smart man. He can figure it out and do the right thing, I'm sure of it."

"Well, there is one way I think you can help him," Aldo said. He held out his hand, and Aaron placed my cell phone in his open palm. Then Aldo passed the phone to me. It seemed too smooth, too quick, as if they'd already had a dry run without me. "Santori is torn up about having to hurt his own flesh and blood. He really doesn't want to do it. He's a lot like you, thinking that if he tries a little harder to reason with Kage, maybe the boy will stop being so hardheaded and listen for once. But the problem is, he's so hung up on you, it's got him blinded. He can't see what's good for him. Maybe if you were to call him and tell him that it was over between the two of you— and make it believable— he'd be able to make peace with his uncle. Santori said the only way he'd give him another chance is if he broke up with you. And since I don't think he's gonna do it himself, I guess it's up to you, kid. His life is in your hands, so to speak."

I looked down. My posture was formal, feet on the floor, hands in my lap. The only thing that gave away my nerves was the fact that I was white-knuckling my phone. I loosened my grip on it and thought about what I had to do. I loved Kage, and breaking up with him was the last thing I wanted. He knew that by now, didn't he? I wasn't sure if anyone could make him believe otherwise, but I was damn sure going to try. I'd give the best performance of my life in order to save his, because I had no choice.

I made the call.

(KAGE)

I SHOVED MY phone into my pocket and stormed out of my apartment, reaching Santori's door in just a few strides and pounding furiously on it.

"Open this door, motherfucker! I know you're in there!" When there was no answer, I let him know just how serious I was. "You've got ten seconds, before I tear my way through this door, old man. And God help you when I do."

On the count of five, I already had images of his body crumpled and bloody from the beating I was going to give him. My adrenaline spiked deliciously just thinking about it. I was almost disappointed when, on the count of nine, the bastard clicked the lock.

"Michael." Santori stood there holding a full glass of red wine. He didn't open the door all the way, but rather filled the opening with his body and leaned against the door edge, his hand anchoring it in place at the top. My uncle always looked evil, with his smug smile and dead eyes. But in the aftermath of the hypnosis session, now that I'd regained my memories, he'd officially graduated from demon to devil. All I could see when I looked at him now was the leer he'd donned seventeen years ago as he taunted me into killing my own brother in cold blood. The phantom flavor of pistachio ice cream flooded my mouth, and I nearly vomited.

"What have you done to Jamie?" I demanded in a strained voice.

Santori's eyebrows drew together in an Oscar-worthy expression of bewilderment, and he slowly tipped his glass up and took a sip of wine. "Michael, I have no idea what you're talking about. I haven't done a thing to that boy. Though he's enough of a nuisance, I probably should. He's attempting to singlehandedly ruin your life, and by association, mine. I'm not accustomed to just standing by and letting people ruin my life. Typically, I do something about it."

"Like what?" I reached out and pushed the door open, catching Santori off guard. He wasn't quick enough to stop me, though I could tell he wanted to. The inside of his apartment was so sterile it was hard to believe anyone actually lived in it.

"I'm busy, Michael, and I don't have time for your drama tonight. Can't we talk about this another time? Perhaps you could make an appointment." His affected boredom didn't ring true. Something was definitely up with him.

"No, we can't talk about this another time. We'll talk about it now. I know you did something to Jamie— got to him somehow. He just called me and told me he doesn't want to see me anymore, and I know he wouldn't have done that of his own free will. This reeks of Peter Santori."

"I told you I don't have time for your bullshit, Kage." Warning bells went off in my head. His irritable tone and the fact that he'd called me by my middle name were visible cracks in his flawless facade, letting me know without a doubt that I was getting to him. For once, Peter Santori was losing his cool, and that was not a good thing when Jamie's wellbeing was involved.

When he laughed a hollow laugh and pushed me toward the door, I pushed back. "I'm not going anywhere until you give me some answers."

"What was the question?" he huffed, stepping aside so that I could move farther into the room.

"Where the hell is my boyfriend?"

Santori rolled his eyes, just as he rolled the thin stem of his wine glass between his thumb and forefinger. He was nervous.

"You slimy piece of shit. I swear on my mother's grave, if anything has happened to him, I'll fucking kill you. I'll snap your neck and piss on your worthless corpse, and watch every second as your dead eyes turn gray. I'll smile the whole time, you fucking sick bastard." I realized that my voice had gradually gotten louder and stronger, and that I'd backed Santori halfway across the room. His legs came up against the glass coffee table, and he sat down on it with a thump. I looked down at him, and he cowered. The most brutal man I'd ever known, a psychopath of the highest order who was afraid of nothing and no one, was cowering in fear of me.

And I thought, what kind of monster does that make me?

195

"You remember," he whispered.

"I remember." My nose was nearly touching his, and I had a buzz— from adrenaline and the heady scent of fear coming off of him.

He glanced down, and I thought I saw his lips quiver. His hands clasped and unclasped in his lap. "I had hoped you'd never find out. Whatever my part in it— I know it was awful. We'd been drinking, and things got… out of hand. I didn't understand the danger. And then for you, sitting there holding your brother, thinking he was going to wake up… I tried to make it up to you. Haven't I given you a good life? Everything you ever wanted. You're the only family I have. My *son*. Heir to everything I own."

I shook my head, trying to sling away the confusion he was causing. He was the devil. He was right about giving me a good life. But money couldn't buy back my brother or wash away the guilt I would feel until the day I died.

"You tricked me. You lied, all those years. Paid people to make sure I didn't remember."

"It would have destroyed you, Michael. We had to make you forget. It was the only way you could ever have a normal life. Please, I thought I was doing the right thing." His eyes were wet with tears, his face contorted. I'd never seen remorse on his face before, but this was it. "Hardness begets hardness, Michael. To be soft is to be weak. My father raised me to be strong, and I've given you the same gift. Strength is what makes gods of men. Don't let a warm body and the promise of love be your downfall. Someday when you're older and this infatuation has passed, you'll realize there is no such thing as love… only respect. And to command respect you can't show any sign of weakness. Just look at yourself. My brother never could have given you the kind of upbringing necessary to shape you into a great man, but I could, and I did. Think about your training and your career. I've been shaping you from the beginning, molding you into something extraordinary. Hardness begets hardness. You are a god, Michael. We... are gods."

"But I killed my own brother. How the hell is that powerful, or extraordinary, or godlike?"

"It's the very definition. Just look in the history books, and even in the Bible. Our struggle has been played out time and time again: brother against brother. It's evolution. It's survival of the fittest, and you and I are the winners."

I just stared down at him, trying to get a handle on what he was telling me. My mind kept hanging up on one phrase: *you and I.* Because if Santori and I were the winners in the age-old, evolutionary struggle of brother against brother...

"Did you kill my father?" I'd asked the question before the thought had even fully taken shape in my mind.

He didn't give me a straight answer. "There's something I need to show you," he said. "Something your father left you. I've been waiting until the time was right, and I suppose that would be now."

"What is it?" Suspicion and excitement warred within me. Why had he not shown me before? What reason could he possibly have for waiting?

"May I stand?"

I stepped back, allowing him to get up from the coffee table and walk into the bedroom. The light was off, but he didn't turn it on. I watched him from the living room.

He pulled an item from the bedside table and started toward me, clutching it in both hands. "I should have already given this to you," he said, pushing it out toward me. By the time I saw the flash of light and realized what it was he held in his hands, there were two wired probes sticking out of my chest and I was being pumped with 50,000 volts of electricity.

My muscles locked up, and my body went down. Excruciating pain invaded every fiber of my being, leaving no molecule untouched. But the worst part was not the pain. It was the ability to think coupled with the inability to control my body. I was completely at my uncle's mercy as I watched him lean over me and stick a syringe in my arm. My skin gave like hot butter, offering no resistance as the needle slipped in, the plunger depressed, and the contents emptied into my veins.

I don't know when the effects of the taser wore off and the drug kicked in, but it didn't matter. I was toast. My body lay in a gelatinous puddle on the floor, all of my hardcore training useless. The Machine was gone, and in its place, a viscous liquid thing with the unfortunate ability to reason. I knew what was happening to me. I watched in horror as my uncle got down on all fours in front of me and shook his head.

"Why do you have to be so stubborn, Michael? When I think of the amount of money I've spent on trying to make something of you, it sickens me. You're just like your father, both of you determined to cause trouble for me when all I've ever done is help you. I *made* you, and this is how you repay me? You're nothing but a selfish, spoiled brat. Do you know how many people have had to disappear because of you? Just because you fucking exist? And you've ruined my UFC dreams. And now I have to change my will. Can't leave everything to a dead man, can I? *Fuck*. You've ruined *everything*, all over some mediocre piece of ass. I hope you're happy."

(JAMIE)

AFTER I MADE the call to break up with Kage, I was sick to my stomach. I literally puked all over the warehouse floor. It hurt like hell to say goodbye to the dream that had taken over my entire life and become my everything, but I had to take the threat to Kage's safety seriously. If there was a chance that breaking up with him would save him, then that's what I had to do.

Just knowing that his life could have been in danger was what had me physically ill. After the things I had learned about Kage's past, there was no doubt in my mind that Santori was capable of following through on any threat he made. The fact I suspected he would enjoy doing it made it just that much worse.

Aldo took my phone back and handed it to Aaron, then we left the warehouse. They were supposed to take me to the airport and put

KAGE UNMASKED | MARIS BLACK

me on a plane back to Georgia, but somehow we ended up at the Alcazar instead.

"Quick change of plans," Aldo told me as he opened the limo door. "Santori wants to speak to you."

"Why?" I was alarmed, because speaking to Santori sounded like a terrible idea even on a good day. Throw death threats into the mix, and it sounded way worse than terrible. It sounded like a trick.

"Relax, kid. He just wants to make sure the two of you see eye to eye on the situation between you and his nephew. What's to stop you from calling Kage as soon as you get back to Georgia? I can see his point. He just wants to talk to you and make sure that's not something you would consider doing."

His explanation did work to put my mind at ease somewhat, but I couldn't help wondering exactly what Santori's definition of *talk* was.

We entered the lobby of the Alcazar, and I was immediately assaulted by the familiar sights and sounds and smells. But instead of feeling like I was coming home, I got a sense of foreboding. For the first time since I'd set foot in the hotel, I had the feeling that I did not want to be there.

"Hi, Jamie," Steve called cheerily from the front desk. But the smile faded from his face when he noticed that I was flanked by Santori's goons. I had to imagine I looked like I was being led off to the slaughter. And maybe I was. That was a possibility I had to at least consider.

I gave Steve a solemn nod as I passed by, and Aldo guided me into the elevator with a firm hand in the small of my back. For a moment, I fantasized that maybe Steve would pick up on the threat

201

of danger and call 911. But part of me knew that wasn't a good idea. That I needed to go and find out if Santori really just wanted to talk to me. Because that's probably all it was.

But as I got closer to the penthouse floor, the elevator seeming to climb faster than it ever had before, a feeling of intense anxiety began to swell up and vibrate within my body. It was the strangest sensation, a steady undercurrent, a hum that made me tremble and long for simpler days.

The elevator stopped, and we got off. Santori's door loomed at the other end of the hallway from Kage's door, and I had the sudden urge to slip away from the thugs on either side of me and bang on Kage's door. But if I did that, it would negate everything I had done already to try to save his life. And, as I found out momentarily, it wouldn't have mattered anyway.

When Santori let us into his apartment, looking strangely unkempt and wild-eyed, Kage was in there with him. My first thought when I saw him lying motionless on the floor was that he was dead, and I let out a loud, long wail that I only belatedly realized was coming from me. Then everything took on this stop-motion quality, as if we were all starring in our very own Claymation horror movie.

Santori, apparently unconcerned with my mewling, told us all to sit down. We did, but all I could do was stare at Kage's lifeless form on the floor, his hands tied at his back with something that looked like a necktie. That made me think of the time Kage had used one on me, and my heart ached even more. So many things he and I would never do.

"Is he dead?" I asked, not meaning to. I didn't want to hear the answer.

"No," Santori said with a wave. "He's just very sleepy." Then he turned to Aldo. "We have a problem. I was supposed to give Jamie an injection." He glared at me like I was the most annoying piece of shit on the planet. "But my nephew got suspicious after the phone call. He came in here threatening me, so I had to do something fast. I tased him, and then I used the syringe on him. Only the amount in the syringe was precisely measured to make it look like an accidental overdose— for *Jamie*. Not this big animal. I'm afraid all that dose is going to do for him is keep him incapacitated for a bit. Then he's going to be very angry."

"What should we do, boss?" Aldo asked. "Want me to throw him off the balcony?"

"Of course not!" Santori spat the words out. "All that would do is draw attention to us. I don't want these bodies found anywhere near this hotel. Understand? The Tick-Tock Inn. We discussed this. I'm just waiting for my source to deliver some more of the drug. Then we can get this all taken care of and go back to business as usual. Put it behind us."

I sat there completely sober, listening to them discussing my murder like it was nothing. It was surreal. My brain was whirling the entire time, trying desperately to come up with a superhero plan to save the day, but it just wasn't happening. Kage and I were going to die of overdoses at the Tick-Tock Inn, and no one would be the wiser. It would be chalked up to a wild night of partying, or a lover's pact like Romeo and Juliet. After the Twitter fiasco from a few weeks back, it wouldn't be hard to sell that story. Gay lovers, under the threat of public outing, commit suicide together in a seedy motel. The tabloids would eat it up. Vanessa could play the grieving— and scorned— fiancée. Santori could walk around with a devastated expression and say, *"No comment,"* when asked for a statement. Kage's UFC rivals would talk about what a shocking blow it was to the MMA community, while secretly breathing a sigh of relief that they weren't going to have to face him in the octagon. It would be quite a media frenzy. And then it would die down and be forgotten, leaving my parents to mourn in obscurity. It was almost poetic, almost romantic. And it was *not* going to happen if there was anything I could do to stop it.

I had to guess from the fact that Santori and the goons hadn't even bothered to subdue me that they saw me as no threat. That was a definite point in my favor. It gave me the opportunity to surprise them. Only there was no way I could overpower three men, especially when one of them had a taser, and the other two probably had guns under their jackets.

"If any attention is called to this hotel," Santori continued, "I won't be able to do anything to Michael, though he certainly deserves it after the way he talked to me."

I gasped without meaning to. But dammit, could the man get any colder? He'd just said his own nephew deserved to die because he was disrespectful to him. As if it was just some punishment like standing in the corner. The man truly was a psychopath. I wondered how Dr. Tanner had been unable to see it for all those years, or if she had just been in denial. Money was a powerful motivator, especially when she could pretend she was earning it by helping a young man in need.

Kage stirred on the floor, and every bit of my attention went to him. I tried to drop off of the sofa and crawl to his side, but Aldo grabbed me. It surprised me when Aaron reached down and removed Aldo's hand. "Let him go," Aaron said, and his voice was strange and wonderful in that moment. The only friendly thing in a room full of impending death.

I crawled to Kage's side and curled up next to him, looking into his handsome face as tears started to fall from my eyes. He was so vibrant, so powerful, and he was going to be put down like an animal. He would never fight again, never love again, and never have the chance to get completely past all of the horrible pain he'd suffered in his short life. He was destined to be a shooting star, and it broke my heart.

I reached out to touch his cheek, and he opened his eyes. They were glazed, but there was recognition in them, and love. I'd wanted to see that one more time before I died, and to let him see the love in mine. He should know that he wasn't dying alone, and that I had not wanted to break up with him because I didn't care. It was because I did care.

"They made me call you," I whispered.

He made a small movement with his head that had to have been a nod. I wasn't sure if he was unable to move more, or if he was trying to give the impression that he couldn't.

As we lay there side by side, staring into each other's eyes, there was a knock at the door. Santori got up to go answer it, and suddenly an idea formed in my mind. Or rather it popped in fully formed, because I didn't have time to think.

I planted a kiss on Kage's slack lips, and then I jumped up off of the floor and ran as fast as I could toward the balcony door. There was a commotion behind me as the apartment door slammed. A quick glance over my shoulder revealed Santori following behind me with a syringe someone had just delivered. The balcony door was just ahead. If I could just get out there, I would have some leverage.

Santori had said that he didn't want me going over the balcony. If he was concerned about drawing attention to the Alcazar and, ultimately, himself, then that's exactly what I needed to be doing. I managed to work the heavy glass door open and step out onto the clear balcony, the twin of Kage's. In fact, I could see his balcony from Santori's, and I wondered that I had not noticed Santori's when we were on Kage's. It probably had something to do with being in the throes of passion and fearing for my life. Kage had taken me to a strange precipice that night— the place where the id ruled, and the need to get off trumped the will to survive.

Oddly enough, that experience had served as sort of a training course for this moment. Standing on the balcony waiting for Santori to come and kill me wasn't nearly as scary as it would have been before Kage hung me over the side of his and fucked me senseless. The irony of the situation was staggering when I allowed myself to think about it. That night, Kage had asked me if I would risk my life for him. I'd said yes, and now I was getting the chance to prove it.

Santori got onto the balcony just after I did, but I'd had enough time to hoist myself up onto the side of it. *God, please don't let this backfire.* If I had to, I would throw myself over if it would keep Kage from dying. I just hoped it wouldn't come to that. Because however romantic and heroic I might want to be, in a choice between living *with* him or dying *for* him, I'd take the first every time.

"All right now, Jamie. You need to come down from there." Santori edged out nervously, as if it was his first time stepping out onto his own balcony, and again I had to silently thank Kage for conditioning me to handle this. When it came to nerves, I definitely had the upper hand over Santori. But he had the syringe… and the hired guns inside.

From where I was perched on the railing, I could still see them, standing over Kage and looking unsure about what they were supposed to do with this new development.

"Boss?" Aldo called, unmoving.

Santori tried again to coax me down. "I'm not really going to do anything to you. It's all just been to scare you. I just need you to go away, can you understand that? You're ruining our lives, and I just need to be certain you will go to Georgia and not come back. So I decided to try to scare you."

He tried on a smile, but it wasn't convincing at all. I doubted if he even knew how to smile for real. This was the crazy fucker who had used an ice cream cone to bribe a little boy to kill his brother. I'd be insane to trust him.

But then what choice did I have? I could jump and hope that he'd spare Kage. If I knew it would do the trick, I'd have pitched myself over right then. But at that point, I would have taken myself out of the equation. Kage would be on his own.

While I sat trying to make up my mind what I was going to do, Santori decided for me. "Aldo," he called. "Get out here and help me."

And that's when all hell broke loose. At Santori's order I glanced over at Aldo. He took a couple of steps toward me with a gun in his hand, which officially answered the question of whether or not they were armed. Fantastic. But just as Aldo was passing Kage's body on the floor, Kage spun up onto his shoulder blades, using his bound arms as leverage. In an instant, he had his legs wrapped like vines around Aldo's, and he was taking the man down. Aldo's two-hundred-plus pounds hit the glass coffee table, and his gun went off as glass shattered around him. Kage yelled out some crazy garbled-up war cry, or maybe he was trying to tell me something. Who knows? Whatever it was that he was trying to say didn't matter anyway. I dropped back onto the balcony just as Santori lunged at me with the syringe.

When Kage had described to me how his mind shifted during a fight, allowing his body to perform actions from memory without thinking about them, it had sounded cool. But I hadn't truly understood what he'd meant until that moment. Now I knew.

As Santori lunged at me, I panicked, my heart spewing beats like Uzi rounds. Then everything happened too fast to process. Fate or instinct put me in the perfect position to grab onto his reaching arm, and my body took over. Drills in Judo class that I'd done just to feel closer to Kage now surged to the surface, and I did the right thing for once. It was so smooth, everything clicking into place like it never had in class. Using his arm and his forward momentum, I got under Santori's body just right to execute a perfect one-arm shoulder throw. The syringe stabbed me in the gut as I flipped him around and tossed him right over the side of the balcony.

The fingers of one of his hands grasped and caught on the balcony rail, and for the first time, he looked like he felt something. Apparently fear for himself is what it took to wake his dead heart. Before he could even bring the other hand up to get a better hold on the rail, I balled up my fist and brought it down as hard as I could on his fingers, feeling bones snap. He lost his grip, and I watched him all the way down.

Another gunshot from within the apartment snapped me out of my daze, and I ran, heedless of my own safety, to see if Kage had been hurt. What I saw surprised me. Kage was sitting up, rubbing his wrists where they had been freed from the tie. Aaron stood with his gun drawn on Aldo's lifeless body, a fresh bullet hole in the dead man's forehead trickling blood onto the floor.

"We've got to get out of here right now," Aaron said. "I've got a car waiting at the underground entrance. If we're here when the cops arrive, we'll have some serious 'splaining to do."

"What about this?" I pulled the syringe out of my belly. It didn't appear that any of the medication had been released.

"Bring it," he said. "They don't need to find a needle with your DNA on it. I already grabbed the one he used on Kage."

We got on either side of Kage and took the elevator down one floor to the service elevator, which took us all the way to the basement. True to his word, Aaron did have a car waiting for us, and we collapsed into the back seat, where I was able to breathe again.

"What happened to Santori?" Kage slurred, reminding me that although he had just taken a larger man down and helped save us all, he was still fucked up from whatever drug Santori was planning on killing us with.

"Don't worry about it, babe. I shoulder-threw and hammer-fisted his ass into oblivion. He can't mess with us anymore."

"That's great," he said, his voice thin. "I was so afraid he was going to kill you out there. And then when Aldo took off to help him—" He got choked up with emotion and couldn't finish his sentence.

"Yeah, well there was no need to worry. I was a real badass. I'm thinking about joining the UFC."

"Oh, brother," Aaron groaned. "Now listen to this one. So full of himself."

"I'm just trying to tell my boyfriend that he doesn't have to worry about anything anymore. I'm trying to comfort him."

"You're bragging," Aaron said. "I put a bullet through Aldo's head for him. You don't hear me bragging about it, now do you?"

I gaped at him. "Actually, yes. You just did. That was actually passive-aggressive bragging that you were doing."

"Boss..." Aaron said, leaning around me to address Kage. "Boss."

Finally Kage glanced up out of his drug-and-trauma induced haze and answered. "Oh. Yeah, Aaron. What is it?"

"Never mind. You weren't listening to us anyway."

I rested my head on Kage's shoulder and kissed the side of his neck. "If it's not too soon, I'd just like to mention that I think I just *earned it* for a long time to come. Maybe forever."

Kage leaned his head on mine and chuckled quietly.

"See?" Aaron said. "Bragging."

I lifted my head long enough to give Aaron a black look. "You know, I liked you a lot better when you were a fucking mute."

He huffed and stared out the window as the car hurtled through Vegas, taking us to God knows where. I didn't care where we were going or what was going to happen to us when we got there. Kage and I were both alive, and at that moment, nothing else mattered.

16

(JAMIE)

- Six Months Later -

KAGE AND I were in our apartment in Vegas enjoying a relaxing night in— no drama, no fans, no nothing but the two of us. Just the way we liked it.

Ever since the night Santori died, we'd been waiting for the other shoe to drop. Aaron had taken us to a seedy motel and convinced us to lie low for a couple of days. By the time the police inspected Santori's apartment, all traces of the struggle had vanished. Aldo's body was gone, as were the blood, the broken glass, and the taser. We never saw Aaron again, and Santori's death was ruled a suicide. Kage inherited everything.

As for our relationship, Kage and I had committed ourselves to building a future together. I guess it sort of freaked us out to realize we'd come that close to losing everything, including our lives. I'd finished my classes and moved in to the Alcazar. Steve was thrilled with that. Now it seemed like he was up in the penthouse almost daily, entertaining me with stories of his hot dates. I'd left my friends and family behind in Georgia, but the cool thing about being with a rich guy was that I could afford to go visit them whenever I liked, and we even had plans for a big reunion in Vegas in the near future.

Kage was busy trying to learn the nuances of keeping the hotel running smoothly, and I was helping in every way I could. Our hope was to get to where we were both running the hotel, and then Kage would do his UFC as well for as long as that lasted.

I was happy. Truly happy for the first time in my life. Kage was happy, too, though he was still working out his demons with a therapist. The loss of Dr. Tanner had been tough for him, especially since her body was never found, and he knew her family had never been able to get any closure. He understood better than anyone what that was like. But the new therapist was helping him, and he hardly ever had a bad dream or got depressed anymore. Hell, we were too busy to worry.

"Got something to show you," Kage said, dropping onto the sofa beside me and flipping on the TV. He wasn't wearing any clothes, and that definitely raised my interest. "It comes on in exactly sixty seconds. Just enough time for you to get naked."

I shot him a confused look. "What the heck are we watching? Did you get a hold of our sex tapes?"

"I did, as a matter of fact. Someone sent me the files anonymously. But that's not what we're watching."

"Have you seen the tapes?" I asked, shucking off my pants and standing in front of him in nothing but a t-shirt.

He reached out and grabbed my dick from beneath the edge of the shirt, working me up to full hardness in a matter of seconds. "I have seen the tapes."

"And?"

He stroked me like only he knew how. "And you were fucking hot. I got to watch all over again how I deflowered your virgin ass. And now I want to do a reenactment." He glanced excitedly up at the TV. "Oh, it's starting. Come sit on my lap and let's watch it together."

I glanced at his dick, noticing that it appeared to be already lubed up and slick. "You came prepared?"

He nodded as I slipped my t-shirt over my head and settled onto his lap. He helped to work me onto his waiting cock, and I groaned loudly as I sank down and it filled me up. "Wow, this brings a whole new meaning to TV time around here. I think I feel a *Friends* marathon coming on."

"*Friends*?" he asked.

I shrugged. "They have a lot of seasons."

He laughed. "Well, this is much better than *Friends*, I assure you. Just watch."

He reached around and started to stroke my dick as the show started. I bit my lip and planned on not paying attention. But when I saw what was on the TV, I changed my mind. On screen, Kage sat on a cream-colored sofa in a well-decorated living room set. He was wearing the same outfit he'd worn the night we met— that sinfully expensive suit that hugged his body like a second skin. The black jacket was tossed carelessly over the back of the sofa, no tie, and the top button of his white shirt was loose.

"My hot man," I groaned. "God, you look amazing in that suit." I pushed up into his fist, urging him to stroke me harder.

On screen, a female interviewer sat opposite him in a wingback chair. Grace Howard was her name, and she was a celebrity in her own right— the new Barbara Walters of the sports world. I wondered if I had decided to pursue a career as a sports reporter, how I would have handled an interview with someone like Michael Kage. I'd probably be shitting my pants just to be sitting in the same room with him, but then I was biased.

Grace smoothed her perfectly sprayed blond curls, smiled at the camera, and spoke in her familiar sultry voice. "This evening, I'm pleased to have the infamous MMA fighter Michael Kage in the studio. He's agreed to take the couch and discuss with me his goals, his dreams, and the controversies surrounding his meteoric rise to fame." She turned her gaze on Kage. "Thank you for being here, Michael."

Kage gave her an aw-shucks look that brought a smile to my face. "Thanks for having me, Grace. And you can call me Kage. Everybody else does."

"All right, Kage…" Grace grinned, clearly charmed by her handsome guest.

And there was that little pang of jealousy that I always got when I watched him charm someone who wasn't me. He was just so damn good at it, I guess I always wanted to be the one on the receiving end. "Eat your heart out, bitch," I muttered under my breath, and Kage squeezed me hard enough to hurt. In response, I squeezed his dick with my ass and made him groan.

On the TV, a very poised Grace Howard smiled at Kage. "So I think the first question I should ask is, how did you get into fighting?"

Kage shifted in his seat. Most people probably wouldn't notice his discomfort with the question, but I did. I knew how he felt about his past. How he wished it didn't exist. I knew there were probably some details he had remembered that he hadn't shared with me yet, but I figured in time he'd trust me enough. At least I hoped he would. No one should have to shoulder such a heavy burden alone.

"I've been into martial arts since I was a very young boy," he said casually. "My family got me lessons, groomed me to be a fighter, so it's all I've ever known."

I smiled over my shoulder at him. "Well played, Kage. No lies, but you haven't given them anything."

"It's been said that you got your start fighting underground," Grace said. "What exactly does that mean?"

"Well, it's not as dramatic as it sounds. A few years back, my uncle issued a challenge, got the word out in the gyms around Vegas. Basically, he said if anyone can beat my nephew, I'll give you ten thousand dollars. Guys came to challenge me. They lost. We fought in a converted warehouse with an octagon in it. It was a private thing with a very small audience, basically just my people and their people. Over time, as my reputation grew and nobody wanted to fight me, the offer got bigger and bigger. Just before I got signed to the UFC, the offer was a hundred thousand dollars." Kage smiled like it was no big deal to issue a hundred-thousand-dollar challenge.

Grace's eyes widened. "And no one ever beat you?"

Kage shrugged. "Nope."

"And did you fight any well-known fighters?" Grace asked.

"Oh, yeah. Sure." Kage said. "Most people don't know this, but by the time I got to the UFC, I'd already fought a lot of those guys. It's hard to pass up a big offer like that, especially if you're one of the best. You think, *Yeah I can win that easily. No problem.*"

"But they didn't." Grace said.

"No, they didn't."

"And why do you think that is?" she pressed.

"I guess you could say I'm determined. I don't really stop, you know? Even when I'm down, I never stop."

Grace nodded. "And is that why they call you the Machine?"

Kage smiled. "Yeah. That, and I'm good at calculating moves. I don't know if it's because I've been doing it for so long, or if it's something that I was born with, like an ability or something, but... I can see things. When I look at other people, I can see what they're gonna do, and I can see what I need to do to counter it. It's kinda weird, I guess. Hard to explain. My trainer Marco calls it bionic eyes." Kage laughed self-consciously.

"Marco does call it that," I said under my breath. It was surreal watching someone whose life I knew so intimately doing an interview on my television. Not to mention having him sheathed in my ass while he watched it with me.

On TV, Kage leaned back a little on the couch, stretching his torso in that seductive way of his, and I wanted so badly to reach out and touch the on-screen version of him. More than that, I wanted to claim him publicly. I wanted to get between him and every person out there in TV land who was watching him with fevered eyes and say, "*This is mine. Don't even think about it.*"

But I couldn't do that. Not until Kage decided once and for all that it's what he wanted. Ours was a game of duck and cover, of takedown and scramble. So far, we had refuted every whispered accusation with a plausible explanation, while avoiding telling lies that would set us up for a big fall if our relationship were ever publicly revealed.

Thanks to Kage's notorious visits to Georgia, everyone in my close group of family and friends already knew the truth about us, so there was no sense trying to hide from them. They had all been sworn to secrecy, but who knew whether that would hold up. You never knew where human beings were concerned. Flash some cash or get them drunk, and they'd sing like Mariah Carey.

"I know you don't like to talk about your uncle much, but I just wanted to ask how you're holding up after his death. That had to have been rough, losing the only father you ever really knew."

Kage smiled. "Inheriting a fortune certainly helps in dealing with the pain," he said. "But yes, it was very tough, and I'm doing fine now. Thanks for asking." He was so sincere. No one would ever have guessed what really happened. That Kage and I were both murderers now, and we were glad Santori was gone.

After a couple more interview questions, which Kage handled smoothly and with his usual charm, Grace scooted forward on her chair and leaned in toward him. The sympathetic crease of her brow and the new intimate posture she'd adopted had me sitting forward on my own seat, which in turn prompted Kage to pound a few thrusts up into me. I wondered if we'd be able to make it through the rest of the interview without breaking down and fucking, because I had already lost my concentration several times.

"Kage, there's a question I wanted to ask you tonight. A question of a profoundly personal nature." Grace's voice dropped dramatically. "I think you know what that question is."

Kage stretched out even further in his seat, conveying a level of comfort that most people would find difficult or even impossible to achieve at all on national television, much less when they've just been told they're about to have to answer a tough question. But then Kage, ever the fighter, was at his best when he was challenged. Like he'd just told Grace, he never stopped fighting, even when he was down.

He gave her a cocky half smile. "Yeah, I'm well aware of the insinuations that have been floating around about me for a while now. I also know that most of these guys talking shit don't have the balls to come right out and say what they mean without hiding behind vague innuendos and silly tweets, so I'll go ahead and say it for them. Yeah, it's true. I've got a boyfriend. Outside of the octagon, outside of this business, he's my world. Nobody even comes close. Some people think there's something wrong with that. I don't. If you look around at these other fighters... Cristiano Diaz, he's got his girl.

Davi Matos has got his wife and kids. Nick Riker has a girl. All of these guys have got someone to go home to after the fight. They've got their baby, I've got mine: Jamie Atwood. That's who I love. He's the one I go home to at night, and who patches me up after I get beaten down."

I forgot to breathe, and there wasn't even the sound of moving air in the room. Only the TV, and even that was silent for a moment. I think everyone including Grace Howard and the studio employees were all stunned at Kage's admission.

Like me, they'd all expected a denial, or at the very least the usual strategic avoidance of the question. Hell, I was his boyfriend, and I never would have expected him to be that blatantly honest. But my heart was soaring in my chest, because I was so damn proud that he had.

I was so shocked, I'd even stopped grinding on Kage, and he had stopped stroking me, waiting for my reaction. I just sat there, a rapt viewer like everyone else who was watching and trying to process what they'd just heard.

I sank back against him on the sofa and grabbed his hand, winding my fingers around his as we continued to watch in silence.

Grace, a true professional, recovered quickly. "Thank you, Kage, for having the courage to be so honest with our viewers. But what about the people who would say that you're a distraction in the ring, because of fears of sexual harassment?"

"Sexual harassment? What do you mean, like people think I'm gonna be grabbing their ass or something?" Kage laughed, one of those genuine boyish laughs with the dimples I loved so much. "Clearly the people who come up with this bullshit have never had a real fight inside the octagon. What I'd like to know is what man can face off with another man in a brutal, no-holds-barred fight to the finish, and still be thinking about sex? Maybe those are the guys who are losing, I don't know. When I step into the ring, I've got only one thing on my mind, and that's winning. And to win, I've got to survive. I'm thinking about how to get you in an arm bar, how to choke you out, or how to kick you so hard you don't wake up until the show's over and they're sweeping the floors. If any of you guys out there who are scared of sexual harassment think you've got what it takes to shake my concentration, I say bring it on. Or you could just stop making pussy excuses why you don't want to fight me. If you're scared, say you're scared. But don't make it about sex. That just cheapens our whole sport."

The barest hint of a smile broke through Grace's professional facade, but she quickly covered it and continued. "You talk about the octagon, but some have brought up locker rooms, training facilities, other places where one might not be so focused on winning. What do you say to the men who are worried about being in one of those situations with you?"

"What do I say to them?" Kage laughed again, smiled his dazzling smile, and sent a subtle wink to the camera— to me. And my heart melted when he said, "Sorry, guys. I'm already taken."

THE END

Sign up for new release notifications at MarisBlack.com

KAGE UNMASKED | MARIS BLACK

222

MORE FROM MARIS BLACK:

STANDALONE WORKS:
OWNING COREY

SSU BOYS SERIES:
PINNED (SSU Boys Book #1)
SMITTEN (SSU Boys Book #2)
UNDECLARED (SSU Boys Book #3)
INITIATION (SSU Boys Short)

KAGE TRILOGY:
Kage (KAGE TRILOGY Round 1)
Kage Unleashed (KAGE TRILOGY Round 2)
Kage Unmasked (KAGE TRILOGY Round 3)

MARIS BLACK ON AUDIO:
Audible.com

Sign up for new release notifications at:
MarisBlack.com

ABOUT THE AUTHOR

My name is Maris Black (sort of), and I'm a Southern Girl through and through.

In college, I majored in English and discovered the joys of creative writing and literary interpretation. After honing my skills discovering hidden meanings authors probably never intended, I collected my near-worthless English degree and got a job at a newspaper making minimum wage. But I soon had to admit that small town reporting was not going to pay the bills, so I went back to school and joined the medical field. Logical progression, right? But no matter what I did, my school notebooks and journals would not stop filling up with fiction. I was constantly plotting, constantly jotting prose, and constantly casting the people I met as characters in the secret novels in my head.

Yep. I can blame my creative mother for that one!

When I finally started writing fiction for a living, I surprised myself with my choice of genre. I'd always known I wanted to write romance, but the first story that popped out was about a couple of guys finding love during a threesome with a woman. Then I wrote about more guys, and more guys, and more guys. I was never a reader of gay fiction, and I'd never planned to write it. The only excuse I have for myself is: *Hey, it's just what comes out!*

I adore the M/M genre, though, with all my heart. It feels sort of like coming home. I can't quite explain it. I've always had openly gay and bisexual friends and relatives, the rights and acceptance of whom are very important to me, so it feels great to celebrate that. But there's also something so pure and honest about the love between two men that appeals to me on a romantic level and inspires me to write.

Thank you, men. ☺

I currently live in Nashville, TN with my devoted husband (who just happens to be my biggest fan), my three eccentric children, and a hairless cat. Life is good.